The battle ended with Lucia pinned to the mat by Corbett's lithe body.

She fought to block the bombardment of her senses. "Someday I'm going to beat you. When I do, will you give me a field assignment?"

Corbett's sensual lips, enticingly out of reach, twitched into a smile. "I have better uses for your talents." He glanced at the clock. "I imagine you'll need extra time to dress for our…*date* this evening?"

Lucia looked into his eyes and anger mixed with helpless longing. She masked them both with a teasing smile. "A date? Hmm, you're hoping the assassin will strike again this evening, and you can hardly put one of your usual debutantes in the middle of a takedown operation, can you?"

She enjoyed a small s̶   n when he looked tak̶

Call it a ̶   t my first field ̶

Dear Reader,

Once upon a time, there were five talented writers of romantic suspense, diverse in age, nature and style. One day these five writers got the notion to write about a private security agency called the Lazlo Group. (Although nobody seemed to know much about this agency, and less about the mysterious Corbett Lazlo.)

Given that many writers consider writing for a continuity series to be about as much fun as, say, having a root canal, mammogram and bikini wax all on the same day, you might guess this response to the invitation to join them: "Are you insane?"

Naturally, I said, "Count me in!"

Why?

Well, I've had the pleasure of working with these five authors before. Then there was the fact that they let me have Corbett Lazlo's story. The Lazlo Group and its enigmatic founder had fascinated me since they were introduced in the CAPTURING THE CROWN series. Who, I wondered, is this man with no past? Does he even have a heart? What sort of woman could hope to capture the love of so private a person?

The answers, dear reader, lie in these pages. I hope you find them satisfying, and that you may conclude this book with the time-honored phrase, "And they lived happily ever after!"

Kathleen Creighton

LAZLO'S
LAST STAND

Kathleen Creighton

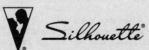

Silhouette®
Romantic
SUSPENSE

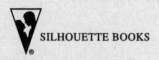

SILHOUETTE BOOKS

ISBN-13: 978-0-373-27562-5
ISBN-10:   0-373-27562-5

LAZLO'S LAST STAND

Visit Silhouette Books at www.eHarlequin.com

Printed in U.S.A.

Books by Kathleen Creighton

Silhouette Romantic Suspense

*Into the Heartland
**The Sisters Waskowitz
†Starrs of the West

KATHLEEN CREIGHTON

has roots deep in the California soil but has relocated to South Carolina. As a child, she enjoyed listening to old timers' tales, and her fascination with the past only deepened as she grew older. Today, she says she is interested in everything—art, music, gardening, zoology, anthropology and history, but people are at the top of her list. She also has a lifelong passion for writing and now combines her two loves in romance novels.

This is for Marie,
and also for Nina, Caridad, Lyn and Karen,
some of the most fertile—yes, Marie,
and cluttered, too, but in
the BEST possible way—minds I've ever encountered.
Thanks for letting me share the ride.

Chapter 1

The attack came in low, but he was prepared for it. He easily evaded what might have been a lethal blow with a feint to the right, and then, in a move as precise and disciplined as a classical dancer's, spun left and caught his opponent in midfollow-through, squarely behind the knees. The attacker, expecting a death-dealing blow to the throat or sternum, went down like a sack of rocks.

Down, but far from out.

Corbett Lazlo had little time to enjoy his moment of triumph. Before he could deal a follow-up blow, his assailant arched his body like a bow and was on his feet again, circling in a half crouch, his eyes hard as bullets, a slight smile playing over his lips. Corbett stood at ease, balanced on the balls of his feet, smiling back. It wasn't a nice smile.

The next strike came like lightning, and, even though

he'd been prepared for it, delivered a glancing blow to Corbett's ribs. There would be a bruise tomorrow. He went down, exaggerating the effects of the injury, and when the follow-through came, he rolled and twisted his body like a fighting cat and came up on top, his opponent pinned with Corbett's knee against his throat. He was now at his mercy; only a slight increase in pressure and the larynx would be crushed. The match was his.

After the briefest of pauses, Corbett removed his knee from the other man's throat, rose and offered him a hand. When both men were on their feet, he bowed respectfully over his own clasped hands and uttered the traditional words of respect by the student for the master.

The other man returned the obeisance, then beamed upon Corbett a wide, delighted smile.

"Bested by my own move! Excellent. It is the moment every teacher cherishes, when the student surpasses the master."

Corbett grinned back, an expression that transformed his austere features in a way that sent a jolt of desire through the woman watching from the screened-off doorway of the dojo.

To Lucia Cordez the jolt was a familiar sensation, as was the ache of longing that came with it. Corbett Lazlo had been the most important person in her life for nearly ten years, but in so many ways he was still a mystery to her—like smoke, she sometimes thought. Visible and real, but emotionally elusive, impossible to grasp.

Careful to keep her feelings well-hidden, she stepped around the carved wood screen and made her own obeisance to the master as he passed her on his way out.

"Ah—there you are." Corbett's features had settled

once more into lines resembling those commonly found on ancient Roman coins. It was his customary expression when looking at her—imperious, impersonal…aloof. "You have news for me, I assume? Might I hope it's good news for a change? Tell me you've traced the source of the e-mails that have been threatening me with so many ingeniously hideous deaths." His tone was light, even a bit sardonic.

Lucia shuddered and said faintly, "Corbett, please."

He paused in the act of mopping his face with a towel to look at her, eyebrows raised. "Oh, don't worry. I'm not the least bit amused by what's been happening. To my organization, to my agents. These breaches of security must be stopped. *Will* be stopped. So? What do you have for me? From the look on your face, I assume it is *not* good news."

She shook her head, biting her lower lip. "I'm sorry, Corbett. Our safe house in Hong Kong was hit last night."

Though she wouldn't have thought it possible, his features hardened even more. His ice-blue eyes looked as if they could etch glass. "Anyone killed?"

She let out a breath. "No. Both our agents managed to escape. But—"

He moved suddenly, tossing the towel away with controlled violence. "Not now. I'll read your report later. Come—" he motioned her out onto the mat with a hand gesture and a jerk of his head "—go a round with me. I want to see if you're keeping up with your skills."

"Now? But—" But it wasn't a suggestion. Even if it had been voiced as one, Lucia knew that from Corbett Lazlo a suggestion was as good as an order.

"Master Liu tells me you haven't been to your last two sessions."

"I might have had one or two other things on my mind," she said stiffly. "Tracing those e-mails—"

"—is high priority, but no excuse for letting yourself get soft." His eyes traveled over her body in dispassionate appraisal.

Soft. She felt the look as if he'd touched her.

She shook off the feeling, gathered her defenses. "Oh, all right. Although," she added in a grumbling undertone as she turned to go to the locker room to change her clothes, "I don't see why it matters, when you won't let me work in the field anyway."

Corbett's voice, sharp as the sound of icicles breaking, stopped her in her tracks.

"I doubt an assailant is going to have the courtesy to wait while you don your workout clothes. Come—as you are. Now."

She turned back slowly, chin cocked in futile defiance. "Not fair. You'll have the advantage." She nodded toward him. He stood relaxed and confident in the center of the mat, feet a little apart, baggy workout pants riding low on narrow hips, arms folded on his well-muscled chest. The way he looked at her, staring down the length of his aristocratic nose, he reminded her of Yul Brynner as the King of Siam, except for the thick silver-streaked mane of hair, the slick of sweat and the patches of red on his upper body where Master Liu's blows had hit home.

His lips curved in a small, arrogant smile. "Then you'll have to fight harder to overcome it, won't you." He made an autocratic cupped-hand gesture. "Come. I'm waiting."

Oh, how she wished her heart wouldn't race so. And *pound*, sending waves of heat into every part of her body. Thankful for the café-au-lait skin that at least partly camouflaged blushes, Lucia locked eyes with the man who was at once the nettle in her garden and the love of her life. Slowly, she reached for the top button of her jacket and simultaneously stepped out of her flat-heeled shoes. Corbett Lazlo's eyes followed her fingers downward, pausing when they did at the cleavage beneath her pale blue silk blouse. Did his eyes flicker slightly, or was it only wishful thinking? She freed the last button and let the jacket drop to the floor on top of her shoes.

As she stepped onto the mat, she felt the thump of her pulse in her throat, heard the rush of it inside her head. And beyond that the quiet voice of Master Liu: *"You must train your mind, as well as your body, Lucia. Your body is only the weapon. Your mind must choose when and how to use it."*

Quiet descended. Her focus narrowed. She saw only a pair of ice-blue eyes, heard only the whisper of her own life forces: blood, adrenaline and that intangible something Master Liu called *chi. I am weightless. Invincible.*

There. The slightest flicker in those diamond eyes. She feinted so that the blow only grazed her side, and her mind ordered her body not to feel it. She whirled and aimed a kick at Corbett's glistening chest, which he blocked easily. She heard a soft chuckle of approval as she twisted around, regained her balance, shifted on the balls of her feet to meet the counter attack.

The battle was short but hard fought. Neither asked for nor gave any quarter, and it ended, as it always did, with Lucia flat on her back, pinned to the mat by Corbett's hard hands and lithe body.

Eyes closed, she fought to block the bombardment of her senses: the crazy rhythm of out-of-sync heartbeats, the scent of clean man sweat, the feel of healthy male hide, warm and slick, salty-sweet to the tongue....

Of course, the last was only her imagination. She fought for the courage to say something flippant and flirty, knowing it was a lost cause. Breathing hard, she had to settle for, "Someday I'm going to beat you."

Corbett's deep voice vibrated from his chest to hers, hinting at a smile. "I'm looking forward to it."

Lucia opened one eye. "If I beat you—*when* I beat you—*then* will you give me a field assignment?"

The thin, sensual lips, suspended enticingly out of reach above hers, twitched the smile into oblivion. "I have better uses for your talents. Speaking of which—" he raised his head to glance at the large clock on the wall above the door "—hadn't you better be off? I should imagine you'll need some time to dress for our...date this evening."

Lucia looked into his eyes, and it was anger she did battle with now—anger mixed with helpless longing. She masked them both, she hoped, with a teasing smile and an airy, "Oh—a date? Is that what we're calling it?"

A small pleat of frown lines appeared between Corbett's black eyebrows. "You are accompanying me to a holiday ball at the British embassy, my dear, in full formal regalia. What else ought we to call it?"

Lucia snorted, deliberately inelegant. "That's only because there've been two attempts on your life in the past few months, and you're hoping the assassin will strike again so the army of agents you have planted all over the scene can nab him. You can hardly put one of your usual…um…*debutantes* in the middle of a take-down operation, now, can you?"

She enjoyed a nice sense of satisfaction when he looked taken aback and didn't reply. Knowing the victory would be only temporary, she seized the moment to twist out of his grasp and regain her feet, pleased with the toned muscles that made the motion as smooth as that of a trained gymnast. *Call it a date, if you like,* she thought as she scooped up her jacket and shoes. *I prefer to call it my first field assignment.*

She slipped around the screen, nearly colliding with the man just entering. Adam Sinclair stepped out of her path with exaggerated care, grinning broadly. "He's all yours," Lucia said tartly, and she sailed out the door with her nose pointlessly in the air.

Adam found Corbett sitting in the middle of the mat, gazing at the screen, knees drawn up, arms propped on top of them.

"She's right, you know," he said to his best friend and long-time partner as he offered him a hand up.

Corbett grunted and stooped to pick up a towel from the mat. "You heard that, did you? How long have you been lurking?"

"Oh, I came in as you two were in the heat of battle—just in time for the takedown, as a matter of fact. Wasn't about to intrude on that little scene. From where I was standing…"

Corbett made a soft sound that in anyone less dignified would be called a snort. "For God's sake, Adam, I'm Lucia's employer, her teacher."

"She's hardly a schoolgirl. Face it, Laz. She's a grown woman, and a damn gorgeous one, at that. And any fool can see she's got it bad for you."

"She's got a bit of a crush, maybe, and if you think I'd be such a bloody jackass that I'd take advantage of that—"

"God forbid!" Adam held up both hands in mock surrender.

Neither man spoke again as they walked together through the maze of gleaming corridors, not until they were inside the elevator, a private one to which only a very few people had access. Corbett pressed the pad of his thumb against a glass plate and gave the voice command for the ninth floor. As the elevator purred silently upward, he said without turning, "Everything's in place for tonight, I assume."

Adam allowed himself a wry smile. "Since you have to ask, I take it you're concerned."

That remark earned him a heated reply. "Concerned? Why on earth should I be? This idiot, *whoever* has been taking potshots at me, must be a bloody poor excuse for an assassin. If he wasn't, I wouldn't be standing here talking to you now, would I?"

Adam shrugged. "You never know, he might get lucky this go-'round—third time's the charm, and all that." He paused, and when no reply seemed forthcoming, added, "In any case, it's not yourself you're worrying about. It's *her.*" He jerked a thumb over his shoulder. "Lucia."

This time he waited out the silence. The elevator gave a discreet *ding* and came to an almost imperceptible stop. In response to another voice command from Corbett, the door opened onto a sparsely but elegantly furnished foyer.

"I can't believe I let you talk me into taking her," Corbett said in a tight voice as he stepped from the carpeted elevator onto gleaming marble.

Adam kept silent while the other man went through the biometric security measures required for entry into his private quarters. "You could always go by your lonesome," he said as he followed Corbett into the immaculate and tastefully appointed apartment. And he was struck by the silence. He wondered, not for the first time, whether the man ever *felt* lonesome.

Adam knew he was one of only a very few human beings in the world Corbett Lazlo trusted enough to let his hair down with, but most of the time even he had no clue what his best friend might be thinking—or feeling. He knew the emotions were there, but they were like rustlings in the shadows, unseeable and unknowable.

Corbett made an unintelligible, though vehement, remark, which Adam could only assume was in Hungarian, Corbett's parents' native tongue. He tossed the towel onto a chair as he made his way to the kitchen. Adam, close behind, heard him mutter, "You're forgetting the reason I'm attending this bloody party in the first place—the *only* reason."

"Ah, yes—Mum and Dad. Right. The M.P. and his lovely lady will be attending, I take it? What about Edward? Too busy with Josh and Prudence's wedding to put in an appearance, I suppose."

Corbett took two bottles of Perrier out of the stainless steel refrigerator and handed one to Adam. He cracked the other open, drank deeply, then smiled and shook his head. Adam knew he still found it hard to believe his favorite nephew—and one of his best agents—was about to marry the daughter of the British prime minister. "Oh, he'll be there. My brother never misses an opportunity to cozy up to the haut monde. My parents naturally will be expecting me to bring a *date.* And I mean, a *believable* date. If I don't, for the next six months I can look forward to a parade of nubile British damsels toddling in and out of my life, each one more lovely and mind-numbingly *youthful* than the last. The strain of keeping—" he swept the hand holding the Perrier in a vague arc "—all this…" He let it trail off.

"Your secret life," Adam finished for him, nodding as he drank. On a different sort of day he knew it would have been dark-brewed German beer, but not today. Not tonight. "Yeah, I can see how that could complicate one's social life a bit. Doesn't have that effect on mine, but then, I've never minded the occasional white lie. One thing you don't need to worry about with Lucia, though, isn't it?"

After a long pause with no reply, Adam leaned one shoulder against the doorframe. "You underestimate her, you know. You trained her yourself—you should know what she's capable of. She's as good as any agent we've got."

Corbett drank the rest of the water in his bottle before he replied. He waved the empty bottle again in a rough half circle, frowning. "Field ops isn't what I recruited her for. You know that. She has one of the most brilliant minds I've ever run across. When it comes to computers—God, I can't begin to understand the things she knows. The things she can do. It would be crazy to risk all that in the field. Insane."

"Yes, it would be insane," Adam said softly, meeting the other man's eyes over his own raised bottle. "To risk…all *that*.

"But," he added quickly, as Corbett's frown darkened, "no worries, in any case. We've got our best people on it, and—" he glanced at his watch "—they're probably in place, or getting there as we speak. Time I was, as well." He set his own empty Perrier bottle on the curved marble countertop and gripped the other man's shoulder as he passed him. "Later, mate. I'll let myself out."

As Adam paused in the foyer to listen to the security system engaging behind him, it occurred to him that it sounded a bit like a cage or prison door locking. These days, with the whole agency more or less under siege, that pretty much described it, he supposed. And what a bit of irony that was, considering how near to the real thing Laz had once come, way back when, during that unpleasantness with British SIS.

Sixteen years ago. God, had it really been that long? Sometimes it seemed like yesterday; then at other times, another lifetime. Hard to believe, now, that anyone in his right mind could have believed Corbett Lazlo guilty of being a double agent. It had been a frame-up, of course, and a damn good one, but still. Even more incredible that he'd been brought up on charges, convicted and sentenced to life in prison for treason, and might be there still if Adam hadn't taken the gamble of a lifetime. Some would have said he was a crazy man to have given up his own job and risked everything to save his best friend.

That's the way some people—most people—had

seen it at the time, anyway. For Adam there had never been any question of a gamble or risk. Stack up loyalty to the service against loyalty to the best friend he had in the world and the man to whom he owed his life many times over… Hell, it was no contest.

Using all the Secret Service tricks and contacts at his disposal, Adam had managed to whisk Laz out of Britain just in time to avoid those slamming prison doors. The two of them had put together an organization of agents, a handpicked few initially, only the very best, people they could trust with their lives. And their first job had been to unravel the conspiracy against Corbett Lazlo and prove his innocence. The latter they'd done in short order. The former…well, that case was still open. And still unresolved.

Sixteen years later that handful of agents had become the Lazlo Group, the most prestigious private-security agency in the world, with a stellar international reputation. Most often they were called in as a last resort, when all conventional means had failed. The Group could be trusted not only to get the job done, but also to be discreet about it. And in exchange for guaranteed results, they commanded top dollar for their work, no questions asked. These days Laz was the acknowledged leader of the group, Adam his right-hand man and still his closest friend. *Friend? More like a brother. Closer than any brother—damn sight closer, for sure, than that prick Edward ever was to him. Hard to believe those two sprang from the same loins. Vain as a bloody peacock, that one, even if he did do a decent job for the Group as the moneyman.*

Although Laz often consulted with Adam before

making decisions about assignments or new agents, Laz's was the final word. As it had been when he'd recruited Lucia Cordez right off the campus of UC Berkeley. And, as usual, he'd been right; the girl was brilliant. And not just with computers. She had the makings of a first-rate agent, and the fact that she was drop-dead gorgeous didn't hurt, either. Fact was, her looks gave her access to places and people not every agent could reach.

Well, they would, if Laz wasn't so bent on keeping her locked up in his ivory tower, too bloody dense to know he was crazy in love with her. And vice versa.

On the other hand, probably just as well the pair of them were as blind as wombats when it came to matters of the heart, Adam thought as he rode the private car down to the subbasement where, via secret corridors, he would switch to the public elevators in order to access the building's street floor. Otherwise one or the other of them was bound to notice Adam was crazy in love with the girl himself.

Lucia stalked across the courtyard, which still glistened with the misty rain that had fallen earlier in the evening. Though, to be honest, to call her progress *stalking* was perhaps overstating it a bit, given that she was wearing strappy sandals with four-inch heels and a gown that limited her stride to something more mincing than regal.

To her extreme annoyance, her escort kept pace with her without compromising his natural elegance one iota.

"I don't see why you should be upset," Corbett drawled in an undertone as, in a seemingly natural gesture, he placed one hand on her back just below the edge of the silver fox stole she wore, wrapped tightly against both nervous shivers and Paris's December chill.

"You might have mentioned it," she shot back, suddenly breathless.

"I thought I just did."

"It would have been helpful if you'd done so *before* I got dressed. I would've chosen something a little more—" she swept a hand downward across her front "—a little less…"

The neckline hadn't seemed *that* revealing when she'd decided on this particular dress for this evening's "date," but now, judging from the caress of the stole's satin lining she felt with each heaving breath, it did leave quite a lot of her uncovered. Again, to be honest, she hadn't been thinking all that much about décolletage when she'd chosen the slithery gold gown. She'd chosen it because the color complimented her tawny skin and brought out the auburn highlights in her hair.

Uh-huh, right. Girl, you chose it because it shows off your booty, and you know you look hot in it. If you're going to be honest…

"You look quite lovely," Corbett said, in the same tone he might have used to inform her she had a smudge on her cheek. "It isn't as though you're meeting the queen, you know—or even the bloody prime minister. Just a minor member of Parliament and his bride— hardly worth getting upset over."

"A minor member of Parliament and his wife who happen to be your *parents*." The last word emerged in a furious hiss. She halted and turned to face him. The horde of butterflies in her stomach turned happy flip-flops at the sight of him, so slim and tall and elegant in his evening dress, the gleaming white of his shirtfront only inches from her own heaving—and now largely uncovered—breasts. She drew a deep breath. "Corbett, you are going to be introducing me to your parents as your, um… They will probably think we…" She paused, met his gaze of cool appraisal, then muttered tartly as she turned to continue her promenade across the courtyard, "Then again, if you're going to look at me like that, they probably won't think anything at all."

"Look at you like…what?"

"Like you're studying a wine list. Or the morning stock report."

"Would you prefer me to leer?" He was there beside her, effortlessly in step with her once again, his expression mildly amused. "Perhaps drool a little?"

Lucia had to quell an urge to kick him. How could he be so completely at ease, when she felt as awkward as when she was queen of the geeks in high school? And as nervous as if the captain of the football team had asked her to the prom?

Before she could think of a witty riposte, Corbett said dryly, "Don't worry, my father will do enough of that for both of us. Well—probably not the drooling." Then his hand was on her back again, touching her in a way he probably meant to be courteous or reassuring, and his laugh held more warmth and genuine amusement than she'd ever heard in it before. "Don't worry, I'm joking. I seriously doubt the Honorable Andre Lazlo will be undone by a bit of cleavage."

Lucia tossed him a look, incapable of coherent

speech or thought now that he was touching her again. He smiled back at her, his austere features romantically shadowed by the courtyard's security floodlights. "Never mind, my dear. You'll understand, once you've met my mother."

Nodding to the footman dressed in Dickensian costume, Corbett took Lucia's gloved hand and deftly tucked it into the crook of his elbow. He added in an ominous tone, "You would probably be wise to steer clear of Edward, however."

Lucia had visited the Paris offices of the British Embassy several times on various errands for the Lazlo Group, but this was her first visit to the ambassador's residence, the grand old building on the rue du Faubourg St Honoré. She barely had a moment to appreciate the spare but elegant entry hall, with its patterned marble floor, red velvet draperies and sweeping curved staircase, before yet another footman was there to relieve her of her stole. She felt decidedly more vulnerable without it. *It's a mission. It's what he trained me for. I can do this.* She lifted her head high and pasted on the confident smile she knew Corbett expected from her.

She was less successful in controlling the tremors inside.

Corbett was aware of the quiver. Slight though it was, he felt it unmistakably even through his jacket and shirtsleeve. He was on the verge of saying something reassuring, but thought better of it. He was the one from whom she was trying so hard to hide her nervousness; she'd hate that he'd noticed.

He felt twinges of protectiveness to her and reminded himself that he'd trained her well, she had no reason for jitters.

That gave way to compassion. Anyone might be a bit nervous at the prospect of meeting the parents of the boss on whom she had a slight crush.

Then guilt: *It was wrong of me to use her like this. Isn't fair to her.*

Although, damnation, he'd been careful to treat her with absolute decorum. Damned hard to do, too, when she was so incredibly beautiful. He could smell her hair, her skin, her own signature fragrance, that sweet, sassy scent that always made him think of warm tropical nights. *Jasmine, perhaps?*

"Dahling! *There* you are. Vere have you been, *édes fiú?* You terry-ble boy!"

The voice he both adored and dreaded soared across the crowded ballroom like the cry of an eagle. At his side, Lucia gave a start and threw him a look, half query, half alarm.

"That would be Mother," he said resignedly, "obviously channeling the Gabor sisters."

Lucia braced herself to meet the couple sweeping down upon them. To her the Honorable Andre Lazlo and his wife seemed to belong to another age, and the chamber music rising above the hum of genteel conversation a fitting accompaniment for them as they glided over the gleaming parquet floor. Lydia-Maria didn't need a towering powdered wig, panniers and a black beauty spot artistically applied to her heart-shaped face in order to fit perfectly with the grand ballroom's eighteenth-century splendor of carved paneling and gilded mouldings, cascading chandeliers and red velvet draperies. In her platinum pouf and shimmering white gown, with a neckline that plunged dangerously close to the limits of decency—*Yes, Corbett, I see what you meant!*—she seemed to glitter like the brightest diamond in a rococo setting.

Her husband, by contrast, seemed almost austere in his tux, even with a festive swath of red, white and blue ribbon across his chest. He was a tall man, regal in bearing, handsome in an ascetic sort of way, with silver-white hair and luxuriant moustache to match, and the ice-blue eyes he'd bequeathed to his younger son.

This is what Corbett will look like when he's old, Lucia thought.

It gave her an odd feeling, as if she'd been allowed a tiny peek behind his facade.

She could almost hear the elder Lazlo's heels click together as he took her hand and bowed over it with military precision, but was unprepared and had to stifle a nervous giggle when he kissed her hand and in the process let his eyes linger on her half-exposed bosom with an unmistakable twinkle of appreciation. She wanted, but couldn't quite bring herself, to look at Corbett, to see if he'd noticed.

The introductions had barely concluded when Lucia saw Edward Lazlo heading toward them through the crowded ballroom, with pauses for handshakes and backslaps along the way. Glad-handing, Lucia's father would have called it, like a politician on the campaign trail.

For all his charm and apparent popularity, Lucia had never managed to like Corbett's older brother. Being around him gave her a feeling of clammy distaste, as if she'd inadvertently touched something slimy and cold. And, since she was the agency's computer tech and he its controller, she had to spend a good bit more time in his company than she liked. She tried her best to hide the way she felt, of course, knowing how close the two brothers were. Knowing, too, that Corbett felt deeply indebted to Edward for financing Adam Sinclair's efforts to clear him of the treason charge, back in their SIS days.

Hard to believe the man could ever have been guilty of so selfless and noble an act, she thought now as she endured his arrogant smile, the look of heavy-lidded appraisal as he took in her gown and cleavage, and the touch of his fat hand on her bare shoulder with a murmured, "How nice to see you, Lucia."

Then for a while she slipped willingly into fifth-wheel status, wearing the stiff, meaningless smile of the outsider as she watched the four Lazlos draw together and become family. Corbett, of course, drew most of her attention; it was fascinating to see him in this context for the first time. She'd always been struck by how different the brothers were, but now she could see how and why that could be so. Corbett took after his father, both in looks and manner, while Edward favored his mother in much the same way. His body was shorter, softer and rounder than his younger brother's, which was all sharp angles and hard planes, like his father's. Edward's face had the open, friendly plumpness of a happy cherub, while Corbett's finely chiseled features seemed always veiled in shadows. And yet, watching, she could see genuine affection between the two brothers, as well as the deep respect both had for their parents.

Families, Lucia thought, suddenly missing hers. She was an outsider here, as she would expect to be. What gave her an unexpected pang of loneliness was the realization that she would be just as much an outsider in her own family now. She'd missed them terribly when she'd first moved to Paris, but over the years, visits to her parents' home in the San Francisco suburb of Pleasant Hill had grown fewer and farther between. Now, on those rare trips to California, all she could think about was getting back to her apartment in Paris, her job…and Corbett. This was her home now, and the Lazlo Group was her family.

And the Lazlo Group—*my family!*—was being threatened. Someone was picking off their agents—*my brothers and sisters!*—one by one. Someone had tried twice to kill its founder and head, Corbett Lazlo. Someone was bombarding agency computers with horrifying e-mails.

And she'd been powerless to stop them.

The hum of genteel conversation, the tinkle of chamber music, the laughter and lights and Christmas cheer all faded into nothing as Lucia's mind tugged and plucked at the puzzle knot that had frustrated her since midsummer. So far all her best efforts had done was teach her that it was far easier to be a hacker than to catch one.

Maybe, she thought, *if I backtrack through…*

"Hmm…are those pixels I see in your eyes, my dear?"

The quiet voice so near her ear gave her a start. Electric currents ran wild across her skin as she looked into Corbett's brilliant blue eyes.

"Let's not keep the ambassador waiting. Shall we?"

She laughed to cover her shiver and tucked her gloved hand into the crook of the arm he offered.

It was an hour or so later, maybe two—Lucia had lost all track of time—when she and Corbett left the embassy's heavily secured courtyard and began to stroll along the rue du Faubourg St Honoré. They walked slowly, close together, like lovers reluctant for the evening to end. The night had turned cold and raw. There were few people on the streets, though by Paris standards it wasn't late. A nasty little wind riffled Lucia's hair and curled freshly around her neck and under her skirt. She moved closer to Corbett's side, telling herself it was permissible to do so, that they were supposed to look like lovers, after all. And she tried not to enjoy too much the warmth and closeness of his body, the smell of his jacket and aftershave.

A little ripple of something—perhaps a combination of pleasure and suspense—shivered through her. As if he'd felt it, Corbett pressed her arm, the one that was tucked through his, closer against his side, an odd little hug that may have been only encouragement but somehow felt more intimate than that.

"You did very well tonight," he murmured, and his voice wasn't soft like a lover's, but had a slight rasp to it, as if the words didn't come easily. "Handling— ah…dealing with…meeting my parents."

She glanced up at his profile and saw the crease of a wry smile in his cheek, even as his narrowed eyes roamed the street and sidewalk ahead, missing nothing. "I thought they were wonderful," she said sincerely, then shrugged. "Your mother especially. She seemed much younger than I know she must be. Your parents would be in their seventies, right? I assume—"

"Mother is seventy-six," Corbett said. "My father will be seventy-nine in February." He glanced at her, smiling that same wry smile. "By the way, I thought you did an admirable job of not bursting into a fit of giggles when he kissed your hand."

"I wouldn't have!"

"I was watching your face. You were on the verge, don't tell me you weren't."

"He caught me by surprise," Lucia said with dignity. "And his moustache tickled."

Corbett laughed softly and gave her arm another of those strangely intimate little squeezes. Lucia felt the same shiver, and this time knew without a doubt that it was pleasure.

"I could have done without that little comment he made about me being—what was it? Oh, yes—'a nice, *healthy*-looking vooman. Vith some *meat* on her bones.' What, exactly, did he mean by that?"

Corbett's chuckle now sounded slightly embarrassed—something new for him. "That was a compliment. He approves of you, my dear. In fact—" now he sounded bemused "—they both did. I think—"

Whatever it was he thought was never revealed. He stiffened, put one hand to his ear and seemed to come to attention, like a hunting dog on point. His eyes were dagger points, focused straight ahead, though Lucia could see nothing alarming about the handful of people hurrying along the still-damp sidewalk, heads down, shoulders hunched against that nasty little wind.

"Lucia, go back to the embassy and wait for me,"

Corbett said in a quiet voice as he gently untangled his arm from hers.

"But I—"

"Don't argue. That's an order. Go. Now."

Chapter 2

Lucia went, but with rebellion in her heart, in her soul and in every ounce of her being. Her feet were the traitors; they obeyed *his* will, not hers. She went, but with every muscle straining against the tug of an irrational yearning to stay at the side of the man she loved and face along with him whatever dangers threatened. She went, but with reluctance in every step, high heels scraping unevenly on the damp sidewalk as she paused and turned every few steps to look back.

And so it was that she saw the events unfold in jerky fast-forward, like an old-time movie.

Corbett relaxed only slightly as he listened to Lucia's footsteps retreating back toward the safety of the embassy. He knew she didn't want to go, that she'd have stayed and fought side by side with him, if he'd allowed it. He felt a peculiar swelling of something he couldn't quite identify. Was it pride or something more complicated?

No time to wonder about it now. Adam's voice was muttering in his ear again, calmly and without a hint of excitement.

"Yeah, mate, this looks like a live one...can't tell what he's carryin'. Definitely comin' your way, though."

Corbett pressed the button hidden under his tie and replied quietly, "Got it. Don't move in...wait for my word."

When she glanced back again, Lucia saw a man turn the corner at the end of the next block. A young man, wearing a jacket with a hood. His hands were thrust deep in his pockets and he walked rapidly toward Corbett, not with his head down and hunched against the cold wind, going someplace warm and in a hurry to get there. No—this man's head was up, and even from that distance, she could see that his gaze was fiercely intent. And fixed on Corbett.

In her heart, in her *gut,* she knew this was wrong. *He* was wrong.

Oh, God, this is it. It's him.

This was the assassin who'd already tried twice to murder Corbett. This time...

No. She told herself Corbett had planned for this. That he had backup all over the place. That just because she couldn't see them didn't mean they weren't there. She told herself she couldn't go back, that he'd be furious with her if she did.

But she did stop walking and stepped into the shadow of the nearest doorway to watch.

She wasn't aware until sometime later that she'd also slipped off her high-heeled shoes.

Corbett watched the man in the hooded jacket come toward him. He felt calm, though his heart was thumping like bloody hell. Well, he couldn't help that, could he? Adrenaline was flowing; he felt ready, eager, almost weightless in his anticipation of the battle to come. A smile curved his lips. Not a nice smile.

"Laz...come on, mate." Adam's voice in his ear had an impatient edge to it now.

The distance between Corbett and the hooded man was closing fast. He touched his tie and murmured, "Steady, old man...steady."

Thirty meters...twenty...ten...

Steady...

At point-blank range, the man pulled his hands from his pockets. One hand held a gun. Using both hands, he brought the weapon up, aimed it at Corbett's chest and fired.

Lucia heard the sound of the gunshot. She watched him fall.

It was the last thing she saw clearly. The next thing she knew she was running—*flying*—down the sidewalk toward the two men, knowing as she ran, knowing without seeing, that the assassin was advancing, aiming his weapon at his target's head for the killing shot. Her scream of rage and despair seemed to hang behind her in the Paris twilight like the echoes of a bugle's call to arms.

* * *

Corbett lay on the cold sidewalk and struggled to breathe. Was his heart still beating? He didn't know, couldn't tell. He thought he was alive. He must be, he could see and hear. But he couldn't move. *Couldn't breathe.* Was this how death came?

He could hear the scrape of footsteps coming nearer, hesitantly...his would-be assassin, checking to see whether he was alive. *If he's learned anything from his last two attempts, he'll put the last shot—the killing shot—between my eyes. If I'm not dead already, I soon will be.*

There's no way Adam can get here in time.

This was it, then. His last moment on earth. Corbett closed his eyes and thought of Lucia.

She didn't feel her stocking feet on the sidewalk. She had no idea she'd dropped her stole, or that she'd hiked her gown to her waist.

Your body is the weapon, Lucia....

Her mind was calm, its focus narrowed, locked on her target. All the strength and will of her mind and body compressed into one powerful force.

And she struck.

It's been said no one can swear quite like an Aussie, and in those first few seconds after hearing the gunshot, Adam did his level best to uphold his former country's reputation. As he was running toward that awful sound he kept swinging back and forth between a strong desire to strangle his best friend and the fear the bloody idiot wasn't going to live long enough to give him the chance.

Why had the bleedin' bastard waited so long to give the okay to move in? Had he been waiting for Lucia to get out of harm's way? Okay, he could maybe understand that, but now there was no way he or the others could reach Laz before the assassin finished the job— if he hadn't already. *If I can get to the blinkin' corner, I'll have a clear shot at the blighter, maybe I can wing 'im, at least. If Laz hadn't given strict orders to take him alive... Bloody hell!*

Adam rounded the corner with his gun drawn, his heart in his throat and his lungs on fire. What he saw stopped him in his tracks.

To Corbett it was flashes of color, flurries of motion, bodies hurtling through space, meeting, struggling, falling, the violence too insanely hurried to be real.

What he remembered afterward was the sound. A screech of pure animal rage; grunts and sickening smacks and thumps. A scraping, skittering sound. More grunts and gasps, the sounds of men in desperate combat.

No. Not men. One man, and one woman.

Lucia.

It was his worst nightmare. The woman he realized had a very important place in his life was struggling for hers against an armed assassin. *His assassin.* And he could do nothing. Couldn't move, couldn't even breathe. Could only watch helplessly while the battle played itself out.

Lucia's initial attack had the advantage of surprise. Her flying kick slammed into the assassin as he stood over Corbett's body, the gun pointed down at his target's head…hesitating, inexplicably, although she didn't recall that until later, and was only unquestioningly grateful for the extra second or two that meant the difference between Corbett's life and the unthinkable. His death.

The kick sent the gunman crashing to the sidewalk. The gun flew from his hand and went spinning across the wet pavement. Lucia dove for it, not noticing nor caring that her bare legs scraped the concrete, or that what was left of her gown barely covered the rest of her. All she knew was a fierce sense of triumph when she felt the shape of the gun in her hands, still warm from the assassin's hands.

She managed to twist her body around barely a split second before the man was on her, his full weight pressing her down.

He was strong. Stronger than she was. Bigger than she was. And now he had the advantage, his upper body strength pitted against hers, as he struggled to force the gun from her hands. She could feel it slipping…slipping from her grasp. But now she could feel his weight easing off the lower part of her body as he concentrated all his efforts on retrieving the gun.

Yes—her legs were free! And she brought one knee up, hard, between his legs.

In that same second there was a deafening explosion.

Then everything went still.

For Corbett, hearing the gunshot was a thousand times worse than getting shot himself. His reaction was instinctive; he tried desperately to get up, go to her, see if she was all right. Help her any way he could. He managed to lift his upper body a few inches before crushing pain slammed him back down. He dragged in a breath, and that hurt, too. He gritted his teeth and got out one word: "Lucia…"

"Take it easy, mate. Don't try—"

"Adam—Lucia—I heard…"

"She's *okay*. Can't you hear her? She's the one swearing a blue streak over there. *Lie still,* you bloody fool, don't you know you've just been shot? Point-blank range, too. If it hadn't been for that armor you're wearing, that slug would've put a hole through your chest as big as my fist. Where'd it hit you? Oh, crikey. Damn good thing it wasn't a couple inches higher, it would've stopped your heart for sure. As it is, I'm bettin' you've got some busted ribs, at the very least."

"Yeah…hurts to breathe. Feels like…I've been kicked by a mule. Where the hell's our shooter? Did Lucia—" Corbett grimaced and put a hand over his eyes. He swore under his breath, then said, "Please tell me she didn't kill him. Damnation—we needed him alive."

Adam glanced over his shoulder. "Nah, he's not dead—not yet, anyway. Bleedin' pretty badly, though. Our girl's doing what she can for the blighter." He looked back at Corbett, grinning. "Wish you'd seen her. I've never seen anybody move that fast in my life. She was like a whirlwind—like that cartoon—crazy little guy, that tasmanian devil, you know? Came out of nowhere. Poor sod never knew what hit 'im. Not at first, anyway. Dropped his weapon, they both went for it, and that's when she shot him. Might've been an accident, I don't know. Either way, she didn't have much of a choice, mate, so you'd better not be blamin' her for whatever happens now. You know she saved your life, right?"

"I'm not blaming her…or anybody else." He set his teeth and struggled up onto one elbow. "My fault. Should've given the go-ahead sooner…"

"Damn straight," Adam said.

He's just a kid.

It was the first thing Lucia thought when she rolled the inert body off her. His body was lithe and strong, but slender, slim-waisted, like a boy's. She pulled back his hood and pressed her fingers against his neck. It was smooth and warm, and she could feel his pulse tapping rapidly against her fingers. *Corbett will kill me if he dies. Don't die, damn you.*

But, my God, where was all the blood coming from? The front of his jacket was soaked with it already. She looked around frantically for something to stem the flow, but except for the clothes they were wearing, there was nothing. Her dress was useless, so she rolled the bottom half of the boy's jacket and shirt into a wad and pressed it against the wound high up on his chest. She was so absorbed in what she was doing that it came as something of a shock when she looked at his face and saw that his eyes were open. Fierce blue eyes, wide with shock and fear, and staring straight up into hers. His lips moved, his mouth opened, but no sound came.

"Don't try to talk," she said, forgetting he probably wouldn't understand English.

But he was still struggling to get words out, so she leaned closer. And heard, garbled but unmistakably in English, "Don't…want to die…"

She lifted her head and yelled, "Adam—I need help!"

She heard Corbett say in a grating voice, "Go on. I'm fine. We can't…lose him. He's the only lead we've got to…whoever's responsible for this damned vendetta. We have to get him to our medical facility. Can't let the French authorities—"

"Too late, mate," Adam said.

Lucia heard it then, too—the raucous seesaw braying of incoming emergency vehicles, so markedly European and so different from the wail of sirens she had grown up with in the States. She saw Adam and Corbett exchange looks of helpless frustration, and she knew the other agents on the spot had already melted away into the night. She became aware of shouts and running footsteps. Embassy security reached them first, along with the few pedestrians out in the chilly evening. People crowded around the four of them; hands reached to offer aid and comfort. Lucia looked down one last time into the terrified eyes of Corbett's would-be assassin, and with a small sob of gratitude, gave her desperate fight to keep him from bleeding to death into more capable hands.

Time passed. It could have been days or minutes, for all Lucia knew. She spent it in a dreamlike state where time could stretch or compress without rhyme or reason. An eternity filled with the press of people and the cacophony of voices giving orders, asking questions, demanding one thing or another all faded seamlessly into the quiet efficiency and muted murmurs of medical personnel in a well-equipped emergency van. Over her strenuous protests she was checked for trauma, treated for shock and released; then, in another blink of an eye, she'd found herself transported through time and Paris streets to a hospital waiting room where, in the manner of such places the world over, time seemed to pass with the speed of glaciers.

At some point Adam joined her, bringing her strong bitter coffee in a foam cup. She sat and held it, warming her cold hands while two policemen came and questioned them about the shooting.

Just a formality, they assured her. It was clearly a case of attempted robbery gone wrong, and witnesses all seemed to agree that Lucia had acted in defense of her own life and her escort's, and that the shooting of the would-be robber had been accidental, taking place in the course of the struggle for control of the gun.

"Zere is just one sing I do not understand," the older of the two policemen said in his heavily accented English, as he tucked his notebook and pen back into his pocket. "Do you know ze reason why Monsieur Lazlo was wearing body armor? Was he expecting some kind of trouble?"

"No, I don't," Lucia whispered. Then she cleared her throat and added in a normal voice, "Corbett *is* a bit eccentric...."

Adam grinned. "Rather like what's 'is name— Howard Hughes, I guess, eh? Or Michael Jackson."

"Not at *all* like Michael Jackson," she retorted, turning to glare at him, and the younger policeman chuckled.

"Zere is just one sing *I* do not understand," Lucia said to Adam sotto voce after the two law officers had departed. "Your story about being a passerby who just happened to witness the incident and stopped to help seemed to satisfy them all right, but I happen to know you had a gun. What on earth did you do with it?"

He gave her an enigmatic look, then after a moment relented. In a seemingly casual movement, he lay one ankle across the opposite knee and gave his pantleg a twitch—just enough to reveal the holster strapped to his leg. He muttered out of one side of his mouth, "Cops'd have no reason to pat down an innocent bystander who's just tryin' to be a Good Samaritan, now, would they?"

Lucia began to laugh, silently at first, with one hand over her eyes. When, to her shock, the laughter became a sob, she clamped the hand over her mouth, but it was too late to stop it. She gave Adam one brief, horrified look, then closed her eyes on the streaming tears. And after a moment she felt his hand come to rest on her shoulder, then begin to pat her, awkwardly, tentatively. The rather touching sweetness of the gesture turned the tears back into watery laughter.

She dabbed at her cheeks with the blanket the emergency medical team had given her, since what was left of her gown was a bit gory and left a good deal of modesty to be desired. She had no idea what had become of her fur wrap and shoes.

"Sorry, luv, haven't got a hanky, I'm afraid." Adam didn't know whether to be relieved or disappointed she'd turned off the waterworks. Not that he minded being cast in the role of comforter, but his usual methods of dealing with female tears seemed far too dangerous in this particular circumstance.

"That's all right." She sniffed, blew, wiped, then asked, "How soon will we know something?"

"Haven't a clue. But no worries, Laz is gonna be fine. He's just got some busted ribs. They're probably running tests and monitoring his condition to make sure there's no damage to his heart. He took a pretty good hit to the chest, you know. Bullets can do some damage, even with a vest on. Believe me, I know."

She just looked at him for a moment with those aquamarine eyes of hers—reminded him of the color of the water off the Great Barrier Reef from the air—then said in a voice he could barely hear, "I know all that. I was asking about the boy."

Adam actually rocked back a bit when she said that, as if she'd gobsmacked him. "The boy—you mean the *shooter?* You're askin' me about the devil that almost killed—"

"He's not a devil, Adam, he's not even a man. Didn't you see him? He's just a kid."

"Yeah, a kid with a bloody big *gun.*" He couldn't believe what he was hearing. Could he be wrong about her feelings for Laz after all?

"Corbett didn't want him dead," she went on in that hushed, almost fearful voice. "What if he dies, Adam? What if I killed him? Corbett's going to be so angry with me."

He snorted. "I seriously doubt that. Especially considering the alternative."

"The…alternative?"

"Yeah—you dead instead of 'the kid.'" He shoved himself to his feet, because he felt as if some sort of giant spring inside of him was getting ready to let go. "Look— you stay put. I'll go and see what I can find out, okay?"

All he knew was he had to get away from her before

he said or did something that was going to embarrass the hell out of both of them.

He found Corbett in a curtained cubicle, hooked up to a monitor of some sort and looking none too happy about it.

"Thank God," he growled when he saw Adam. "I was about to abandon all hope of rescue. Help me up, will you?"

Adam was about to question the wisdom of that move but changed his mind when he saw the look on Corbett's face and instead simply offered his arm.

Corbett gripped it hard, gritted his teeth and got himself hoisted up into a sitting position and turned with his legs hanging over the side of the gurney. "I don't know why they insist on all this—" he waved a hand at the wires attached to his arms and chest "—for some broken ribs and one hell of a bruise. It doesn't require a medical degree to tell me I'm going to be damn sore for a while."

"Yeah, you are. So you sure you want to be doing whatever it is you're about to do?"

"Look, I'm going to hurt no matter where I am. I'd just as well do it at home. At least there I can—" He broke off, swearing under his breath, to glower at Adam. "Fill me in. How's Lucia? Is she—"

"She's fine—a bit shaky, but she'll be okay. She's here, by the way—out there in the waiting room. Worried sick about the shooter, if you can believe it. Worried she's killed him. Thinks you're gonna be cranky with her if she did."

Corbett jerked and managed to whisper, "Good Lord," through the resulting hiss of pain.

"Yeah," Adam said, refraining from any comment that could be construed as sympathy. "I told her it was him or her—not too much she coulda done but what she did."

Corbett's mouth tightened and his eyes got the stony look Adam knew all too well. "What's his condition?"

"They won't tell me much, given I'm not family. All they'll say is, he's in surgery. I'm thinkin' it's probably too soon to tell if he's gonna make it."

"Damn. Bloody mess..." Corbett lifted a hand to scrub at his face. Finding himself still tethered to the monitor, he tore the wires from his arm and chest in a rare fit of temper. "We should have had transport there on the spot, dammit. We should have gotten him out of there before—did we at least get an ID? Do we know who the bastard is?"

Adam cleared his throat. He'd had happier moments facing a dentist's drill. "Sorry, boss. Didn't have time to go through his pockets. Lucia had her hands full just tryin' to stop the blood. If they've ID'd him—" He broke off, swearing, as his words were drowned out by sounds of a commotion of some sort drifting in from beyond the curtain. "What the bloody hell—"

The voice, now risen to clearly audible levels, was French accented, harsh and strident, almost as deep as a man's but somehow unmistakably female. It bulldozed right over the attendant's murmured response. *"I want to see him. Now! He's here—I know he's here!"*

"Whoa, someone's not a happy camper." Adam tweaked aside the curtain to have a look, but the speakers weren't visible from where he stood. He threw a glance over his shoulder. "Maybe I should go—" He broke off, due to the fact that the man he was speaking to appeared about to take a header off the gurney.

"Laz? Here, mate, what—" He managed to get to him just before he toppled over, while out in the lobby the woman, whoever she was, ranted on.

"Tell me how he is, damn you! *Don't* tell me you cannot! I am telling *you*, I *am* his family. I am his *mother!*"

"Are you all right, man? Crikey, you've gone as white as a sheet. Here—lie down." *Bloody hell,* Adam thought. If it was his heart after all… "I'll get the nurse."

"Help…me up, dammit. Got to see…" Corbett's grip on Adam's arm would have done a croc proud.

I know that voice.

It couldn't be. Just wasn't possible. But there was no mistaking it, even after almost twenty years. Corbett could hear its echoes resounding through the halls of the emergency wing, strident, raw, crackling with emotion.

Her voice.

"You will pay for this, Corbett Lazlo! Everything you care about, whatever means the most to you, I will destroy. If it takes the rest of my life, I swear I will… make…you…pay!"

He told himself it wasn't her, but he had to see with his own eyes.

With one arm across Adam's shoulders and the other across his ribs, he managed to stand erect. Dark splotches were floating through his field of vision. He shook his head to clear it…concentrated on breathing deeply. Evenly. *Relax…tensing up only makes the pain worse.*

Bloody hell. He'd never felt so feeble and woozy. Somewhere in the distance he could hear Adam swearing at him, but he couldn't spare the energy it would take to tell him to can it. He needed every ounce of strength just to take those first steps.

Out in the emergency entrance, the woman's voice had quieted to a raspy, throaty sound, like a lioness purring. And Corbett remembered that one, too, as clearly as if it had been yesterday….

Murmuring words of love to me in a tangle of sweaty sheets on a stolen afternoon in the hot little room in Montmarte… Saying my name in a way no one else ever has, before or since, giving it the French pronunciation: Cor-bay…

Speaking of betrayal, as we sat together on a rooftop in London, watching the fog swirl around the chimney pots, with that particular intensity in her voice and in her eyes, that hint of violence and danger that made me wonder sometimes whether she was not quite sane. "I give you fair warning, mon cher. *I love with passion and I hate the same way. Do not ever make me hate you…."*

He'd been young then, and had laughed off both of them—the words of love and the warnings—and he'd known in his heart it was the danger that made her so irresistible.

Just as he knew in his heart *now* that it was not only possible, it was true. The voice was hers. He knew it even before he heard the words that erased all possibility of doubt.

"Yes, that is right. I am Cassandra DuMont. His name is Troy DuMont. He is my son. *Now* will you tell me where… Yes, yes, I understand he is in surgery…."

Corbett didn't hear the rest. The initial shock of hearing her voice, recognizing it, had blocked the sig-

nificance of her words from registering on his con-
sciousness. Now, as he pushed through the double automatic doors into the triage area, he found himself
face-to-face with the woman he'd tried so hard to ex-
punge from his memory. He'd even thought he'd succeeded. Hoped he had. Now he knew how foolish he'd
been to even try. Knew he should have paid more attention to the things she'd said to him, both the love words
and the warnings.

Because suddenly, as if a curtain had been torn
down, he saw everything clearly. All at once he *knew*.
All the months of watching mission after mission end
in near disaster, of trying to track down moles and trace
vicious threats delivered via e-mail, of seeing his agents
picked off one by one—even that mess years ago that
had gotten him branded a traitor and booted out of
British SIS, and would have seen him locked up in
prison for the rest of his life—he knew who was responsible for it all.

Cassandra.

And there was worse than that. Much, much worse
than he could ever have imagined.

"He's my son!"

Cassandra DuMont had a son. A son who had tried
three times to kill him and, but for Lucia and a state-of-
the-art Kevlar vest, would have succeeded. A son now
fighting for his life only a few floors away. A son who
appeared to be at least nineteen or twenty—certainly no
younger. And that could only mean…

He's my *son.*

Corbett stood frozen while the doors to the E.R. area
swished shut behind him, still dazed, caught in a night-

marish web of shock and disbelief. And it was in that moment that she turned and saw him.

It was odd, but with everything that had come crashing down on him in the past few minutes, his brain still managed to register the fact that she was beautiful. Odd, too, that he could notice how much she had changed, and yet was so much the same. The same tall, voluptuous body, the same golden curls, the same big—slightly protuberant—blue eyes. But the years and the thirst for vengeance had taken their toll, too, and in that instant just before she recognized him, he felt a flash of sorrow for the loss of the passionate but somehow naive young girl he had known.

"You!" She shrieked the word and lunged at him, as if she meant to kill him on the spot, with only her bare hands. Adam managed to intercept her before she could reach him, and she stared wild-eyed past the restraining barricade of his arm like a crazed animal through the bars of a cage. *"You* did this, Corbett Lazlo! You shot him— just like you shot my brother. If you've killed him, too…"

"Here, now," Adam said, panting a little as he tightened his hold on her increasing struggles, "I think you've got things a bit backward, haven't you? Your boy was the one doin' the shooting. Tried his best to kill Mr. Lazlo, here."

"Yes!" She hissed it like an enraged cat. "And should have, if he'd only waited for the right moment, as I taught him. If he'd had more patience." Her mouth stretched in a terrible travesty of a smile. "He would have killed you, Cor-*bey*—his own father. *Yes,* that is right. As you have already guessed, the man you shot is your own *son!"* Her voice broke, before it erupted in a

shrill crescendo. "If you have killed him, I will make you wish he'd killed you instead. I will make you pay—"

Behind Corbett the door whooshed open. In the sudden silence, a voice spoke calmly…quietly. Another voice he knew well.

"Madam DuMont, Corbett didn't shoot your son," Lucia said. "I did."

Chapter 3

Corbett felt himself go cold from his scalp to the pit of his stomach. There was a moment when he was literally frozen in place, unable to move, unable to think. Unable even to decide how to feel. On the one hand, he could have throttled Lucia himself if it could have prevented her from uttering those words—words that amounted to her death warrant.

But then again...what was this strange shimmering, vibrating *warmth* now beginning deep inside his chest and spreading slowly through him? Was it *admiration*?

Because, by God, he had to admit she was magnificent. She put him in mind of an avenging goddess, wrapped in an EMT's blanket, barefooted, the torn remnants of her golden gown swirling around her scraped and dirty legs, red-brown curls gone wild as if they had life and energy of their own.

Or was it something else that made his heart quiver so oddly? Something else entirely—perhaps the fear in her deep blue eyes contrasting so poignantly with the determined set of her mouth and the smudges of dried blood on her smooth, soft cheeks…

The frozen moment—and that's all it was, a moment—passed. Movement resumed with an explosion of sound and fury. And after that things happened the way they do during times of disaster—quickly but at the same time seeming to move in slow motion: Cassandra shrieking like a wounded leopard and lunging toward Lucia; Adam brushing past Corbett to intercept her once more; Corbett moving in the opposite direction, moving through the breath-stopping pain in his ribs to grab Lucia and shove her behind him.

Before the echoes of Cassandra's initial scream had died, while she was still drawing breath for a new assault, the elevator doors swished open. A doctor in surgical scrubs, face mask dangling from its neck straps, stepped out. Confronted with the strange tableau in the foyer, he halted as if he'd hit a wall.

Four faces turned toward him, and then once more, all motion, all sound, stopped.

The doctor's uncertain gaze traveled from one emotion-wracked face to another. Paused at Cassandra… focused on Corbett.

"Are you the parents of Troy DuMont?"

And time resumed its normal cadence.

Too dazed to do otherwise, Corbett simply shook his head, while Cassandra DuMont whirled, tearing herself out of Adam's grasp.

"*I* am! I am his mother. Tell me—my son—is he…" Her voice was the terrible croaking of a mother in terror.

"He's still in surgery at the moment," the doctor said in calm, British-accented English. "He's come through quite well, thus far. If you'd care to come along with me, there's a place upstairs where you can wait more comfortably."

Cassandra threw a look back at Lucia. Corbett waited with muscles tense as she hesitated, the battle between a madwoman's thirst for vengeance and a mother's love for her child played itself out, the struggle written in anguish across her face. Then she gasped and bent forward as if she'd taken a blow to her stomach, and began to move backward toward the elevator as if pulled against her will by an irresistible force. In the doorway she paused, made a *V*-sign with two fingers like the forked tongue of a snake and stabbed them at Lucia.

"Chienne! Tu es fichue…"

The words were in French, but the venom in them was unmistakable in any language. *Bitch! You are* dead.

For several seconds after the elevator doors had closed there was utter silence.

Adam broke it first with an explosive laugh. "Always was a charming wench. Did I understand her correctly? Did she say—"

"Later." Corbett's face was grim as he jerked his head toward Lucia. "We've got to get her out of here. Cassandra won't wait for the outcome of the boy's surgery to make good on that threat. How'd you get here?"

"Caught a cab, actually, since the other lads weren't inclined to wait around to give me a lift."

"That'll have to do. See to it, will you?" The grip on Lucia's arm tightened.

As she allowed herself to be steered toward the exit doors, she watched in a kind of numb bemusement as Adam turned up the wattage of his smile and swooped in upon the poor desk nurse, who'd been hovering behind her counter like a mouse behind a leaf, and was looking more confused than alarmed. She stammered a bit as she announced that she'd already summoned security, and blushed when Adam told her cheerfully to cancel that and summon a taxi instead.

Lucia thought it interesting that the girl who'd been steadfast in facing down a wildly distraught mother's demands, seemed completely flustered in the presence of Adam's Aussie charm.

As for her own feelings, they were in such turmoil she felt all but paralyzed. Though oddly, not with fear. It was *anger* she felt, and an irrational sense of betrayal. Irrational, because what right did she have to be jealous of anyone Corbett chose to involve himself with? But jealous she was. And this was even more odd because she'd never minded—well, not *terribly*—the parade of nubile beauties he'd "dated" briefly on and off over the years.

But this? A son?

For there to be such passionate hatred now, she knew, there must once have been an equally passionate love.

The automatic doors whisked open to admit a gust of cold misty air. Its effect on Lucia was like a slap in the face, and while it did nothing to lessen her misery, it did serve to snap her out of her sleepwalking state.

"It *is* December," she said in a voice that matched the

weather, and gazed pointedly at Corbett's chest, which was quite bare and still trailing an assortment of tubes and wires. "You might want to put on some clothes."

She didn't mention her own state of undress, but drew some satisfaction when his startled look took in the thin blanket she was clutching around her. Noting the fact that it didn't come close to covering her legs, and that those legs were clad only in torn nylon stockings.

His mouth hardened and his brows drew inward. Still dragging her with him like a recalcitrant child, he made a swift U-turn and headed back to the E.R. Doctors and nurses immediately surrounded them, scolding and warning in two languages of the irresponsibility and dire consequences of their actions. Which Corbett, of course, ignored, and instead demanded his clothes. A nurse, looking troubled, nevertheless scurried to fetch them. With equal imperiousness, since Lucia's clothes were unavailable, Corbett demanded she be provided with something to wear in their stead. Another nurse hurried to obey.

None of this surprised Lucia in the slightest. It was simply the way things were done with Corbett Lazlo.

A short time later, still clutching the blanket but now dressed in nurses' scrubs and squeezed between Corbett and Adam in the backseat of a cab driven by an apparently suicidal Haitian, Lucia listened to a conversation in which her immediate future was being planned. It was a two-way dialogue, without any input at all from its subject.

"We'll need a chopper," Corbett began as soon as they were seated, destination given and the taxi in motion.

Adam's response was brisk. "Already on it, boss. It's warming up as we speak." There was a brief pause before he added, "I'm assuming a safe house?"

"I don't trust any of our 'safe' houses. There's only one place I know of where I can be certain Cassandra can't get to her."

Tempted to thrust her hand in the air like a first-grader, Lucia cleared her throat and said, "Excuse me?"

"Ah—the old homeland?" This was Adam, as if she hadn't spoken.

Corbett nodded. "It's the only place I can think of that's not on anybody's radar."

"Even mine." Adam again, wryly. "So you'll be wanting the Citation, as well, I presume?"

"Excuse me!" Lucia said, more loudly. "I *presume* I'm the one you're talking about whisking away to parts unknown. Do I get any say in this?"

"No!" Corbett and Adam responded together.

Lucia did a slow, silent five-count during which she managed to swallow her anger and remind herself it was she these two insufferable alpha males were bent on protecting. Though she wasn't entirely clear as to why that was. The revelation that Corbett Lazlo had a son— one evidently bent on killing his own father—had driven all other intelligent thought from her mind.

"Forgive me," she said, when both men seemed to be waiting for her to speak, "I'm trying to understand what just happened. And what it is about this particular woman that has you both turning tail and running for cover like…like—"

"Yeah, mate, I wouldn't mind a bit of explanation, myself." Adam's tone was semiserious, for once. "This *is* the same Cassandra DuMont we know from our old SIS days, right? Daughter of Maximilian DuMont, late and unlamented head of the dastardly organization we call S.N.A.K.E.?"

"Snake?" Lucia said, incredulous. "The organization Dani pretended to work for as the Sparrow?" Dani Moore, a former SIS agent, had recently married a Lazlo Group man, Mitchell Lama. The two had uncovered a disloyal Lazlo Group employee, Chloe Winchester, while on a mission together for Corbett. Chloe had thought Lucia had gotten the job she should have had and had been selling Lazlo Group inside information to the SIS in a twisted revenge scheme.

"Yes," Corbett said. "We got into the habit of calling them that back in those 'old SIS days,' mainly, I suppose, because that's what the bastards were like. Silent and deadly."

"Right-O," said Adam. "You never knew what rock you were going to find the blighters hiding under, coiled up and just waiting for the moment to strike."

"We used to try and outdo each other coming up with clever things for the letters to stand for," Adam said with a chuckle. "'Sinister Network of A-holes, Killers and Extortionists'—that was one of me own, I believe."

"My personal favorite was 'Society of Nasty Auld Knaves and Evildoers,'" Corbett added dryly. "I believe the current SIS meaning is 'Syndicate of Nasties, Assassins, Killers and Evildoers.'"

"I know they're killers for hire. Tell me what your connection is to them."

"They started out as mercenaries. Their leader was Maximilian DuMont. He was a French mercenary in

Southeast Asia during the early days of the Vietnam conflict, before he got a taste of the drug trade and decided it was a bit more lucrative than fighting other people's wars for them. Made a mint of money, and when the Soviet Union fell, he was in a perfect position to expand into the arms business. Recruited a lot of ex-KGB agents who had an inside track to where the surplus weapons were stockpiled. There was a major war going on at the time among all the weapons dealers over who'd garner the lion's share of the spoils. Max and his thugs came out on top, mainly because there wasn't anything they wouldn't do to eliminate the competition, and those competitors knew it. If they valued their homes and families, they got out of Max's way. If they didn't…well, then they probably died along with their wives, mothers and children."

Lucia, though warm enough snuggled between the bodies of two big men, nevertheless felt a chill. "My God. And Cassandra DuMont is this monster's daughter. No wonder—"

"Oh, that's not the half of it," Adam said with gossipy glee. He leaned forward to speak to Corbett around Lucia. "You want to tell her the rest, mate, or shall I?"

"Oh, by all means, be my guest." Corbett's tone was acidic—just short of bitter. Not at all like him.

And which didn't appear to faze Adam. "After a few major arms deals featuring Soviet weaponry were traced back to the DuMont organization, SIS—CIA, too, I should think—got interested. Laz and I were part of the team on Max's trail. We got a bit too close, apparently, because old Max decided we needed to be taught a lesson. Sent his daughter to seduce the lead agent on the case, which happened to be our friend, here."

As Adam talked, Lucia watched Corbett's profile, trying to decipher the tight smile and narrowed eyes in the everchanging light inside the cab. Wanting to understand the tension she could feel in his body, pressed up against her side.

"She was supposed to set him up—to be kidnapped, tortured, murdered—probably all three, based on Max's track record. It was a warning to the rest of us to back off. That was the plan, anyway. Trouble was, things didn't go quite according to Maximilian's plan. You see, Cassandra fell for Laz, arse over teakettle—"

Revelation came to Lucia via the very tiny twitch she felt in Corbett's body, as if he'd experienced an unexpected stab of pain.

He feels guilty. He blames himself for what's been happening…his agents' deaths.

And he shouldn't, she thought angrily. *He's a good and decent man who cares deeply about all his agents. He isn't to blame for someone else's evil. He isn't.*

"—and instead of giving him up to her old man, she warned him. Maximilian never did forgive her. It's a wonder he didn't kill her, even if she was his own daughter. But in the end, I suppose, what he did was worse."

"What *did* he do?" she asked, holding her breath for the answer.

"Disowned her," Corbett replied in a flat voice.

"Cut her out of his organization completely." Adam picked it up from there. "But that wasn't the worst of it. Not long after that, Max's son, Apollo, came gunning for Corbett." He paused, and in the light of the streetlamps they were passing, Lucia saw the shadows in Corbett's face go long and deep. Adam went on in a thoughtful tone, "I never did figure out how you knew just where and when they'd be coming for you. You want to—"

"It's neither the time nor the place. Needless to say, I'm fairly certain Cassandra is behind all my troubles, all of them for the past nineteen years," Corbett snapped.

They were in the financial district now and approaching the ultramodern building that, in addition to the well-known banking institution on the ground floor and several securities and insurance firms higher up, housed the secret headquarters of the Lazlo Group. Corbett moved as if to shift forward and at the same time reached for his wallet. Then he drew a sharp breath and held it, and leaned back instead.

"Got it," Adam said under his breath, and taking out his own wallet, counted out some euro notes to give to the cabdriver.

Meanwhile, Lucia struggled to hold on to her frustration. There were so many things she wanted to know. Felt she *deserved* to know. Particularly since these dramatic events in Corbett Lazlo's past appeared to be about to dramatically affect her future.

"She—Cassandra—said you killed her brother," Lucia said to Corbett in a tight but steady voice. "Did you?"

He replied with a quiet, "Yes."

"The little punk didn't give 'im much of a choice," Adam said as he settled back in his seat. "And that's the plain truth of it. If he hadn't—"

"Not now." Corbett's tone was one that neither Lucia

nor Adam cared to challenge. Adam gave her a smile and a shrug of apology as the cab rolled into the underground parking garage.

Following Adam's directions, the driver, with protesting tires, pulled around to a remote corner of the lot and jolted to a stop. Adam opened his door and turned to help Lucia, both of them carefully avoiding watching Corbett's determined but obviously painful struggle to extricate himself from the car.

"He'll be okay," Adam murmured for her ears alone, and she nodded and mouthed the words, "I know."

But she marveled at the strange confusion of emotions stirring inside her, seeing the indestructible Corbett Lazlo in such a state.

As the taxi drove off with a screech of tires, its three former passengers turned to a door marked in French, in large black letters: Emergency Exit—Authorized Personnel Only. Adam opened the door using a remote and held it while Lucia and Corbett entered what appeared to be a large steel-walled vault, then followed them in, closing the door after him. Corbett placed his palm on a glass panel near the door, and a steel panel above it slid open to reveal a state-of-the-art optical scanner. One by one, each of them stepped up to the screen, eyes wide-open. Only when all three had passed the iris recognition scan did the larger panel slide back to reveal the elevator.

The purpose of this, Lucia knew, was to prevent anyone from gaining access to the Lazlo Group secret headquarters by taking one of its members hostage. Hidden sensors in the vault would determine the number of people inside. Entry could only be accomplished once every person had been cleared by iris scanning. She remembered thinking, when she'd first been introduced to the system, that it seemed a bit excessive—even paranoid. Now, remembering the light of madness in Cassandra's eyes, the way she'd stabbed those forked fingers when she'd spit the words, "*Tu es* fichue…"

A shudder ran through Lucia. For the first time, as the steel-reinforced elevator whisked them silently upward, she was grateful for the extreme security measures and no longer thought them the least bit excessive.

It wasn't until the elevator doors opened again and she found herself standing at the entrance to Corbett's private apartment that it hit her. Wherever in the world she was being whisked away to, it was happening *now.* The helicopter was on its way. It would land on the rooftop of this building, and she would be bundled aboard like baggage, without even being allowed to go home to her apartment to pack her own.

It was, suddenly, simply too much.

As Corbett and Adam stepped out of the elevator, she took a step backward and said in a strangled voice, "I can't— I'm not doing this."

Both men turned to look at her, wearing identical expressions of noncomprehension, as if a piece of their luggage had acquired a voice.

Corbett's expression changed quickly to a puzzled frown. "Can't do…what?"

She was suddenly furious with him. For an intelligent man, could he *be* more obtuse? "I can't just *leave* like this. I have to go home first."

His frown deepened. "I don't see why. Unless you have a cat. Do you? I'll arrange for someone—"

"*No,* I don't have a cat. I have to—" her voice rose as Corbett began to shake his head "—I have to get my *stuff.*"

"Out of the question. By this time Cassandra will no doubt have your place located and staked out. No, we're getting you out of the country—now." He reached for her arm, and she pulled away like a stubborn child.

"Dammit, Corbett, I don't have any clothes."

Adam said quietly, "She's got a point, boss."

Corbett glanced at him, then let out a breath and drove a hand through his already untidy hair. "Oh, all right then. I'll send someone to pick up your things. Adam?"

"On it." Adam had already plucked a cell phone from the inside pocket of his jacket.

As he turned away, mumbling instructions into the phone, Lucia ventured, though still with some reluctance, from the elevator.

"What about my job?" she said to Corbett in a low voice as he was engaged in convincing his security system to grant them entry into his apartment. "I'm so close to tracking down the source of those e-mails. Who's going to—" Seeing the wry smile beginning to form on his lips, she broke that off and said, "Oh."

"Yes, I think we can mark *that* little mystery solved, at any rate," he said dryly. He opened the door and waited for her to enter ahead of him. "I'm only surprised I didn't think of it immediately—the messages did have Cassandra's particularly nasty style. And the attacks on my agents and safe houses… Although to be perfectly honest, I wasn't entirely certain she was still alive. Given the circles she moves in." He paused to frown at Lucia. "What is it now?"

She had halted just inside the door and was looking around, feeling a little like Dorothy, awaking to find herself in Oz. In all the years she'd worked for Corbett Lazlo, all the hours she'd spent in his company, she'd just realized this was the first time she'd ever set foot in his apartment. Her heart gave an odd thump and seemed to drop into the bottomless well that was her stomach. She couldn't put her finger on *why*. Not then.

"Nothing," she breathed, willing herself to relax as she moved through the entry and into the graciously appointed but strangely sterile living room.

Adam came in, closing the door behind him. "Team's ready to roll," he said briskly as he tucked away his cell phone. He turned to Lucia. "You might want to write out a list, luv. I expect they'll be in a bit of a hurry."

Though his glance rested only briefly on her face, which she knew must be a disaster, his nut-brown eyes seemed kind. Adam *was* kind, she realized, in spite of his reputation as a bit of a player. He'd always treated her with a kind of cheeky affection—rather like an older brother, she thought, although she'd never had a big brother and could only guess what that might be like. He was terribly good-looking, too, and she wondered why his company never made her heart do unnatural things the way being close to Corbett did.

"You warned them to be on the lookout for Cass's crew?" Corbett asked quietly, as if lowering his voice could somehow keep the gravity of the circumstances from Lucia. As if she were a child to be protected from the truth.

"You know I did, boss." Adam's grin was wide and showed his rare dimple.

Corbett opened a top drawer in a carved and inlaid sideboard Lucia knew must be a priceless antique, took out a notepad and ballpoint pen and handed them to her. "Make it quick," he said on an exhalation, sounding put-upon.

Lucia's chest felt tight. Everything else—her muscles, her insides, her nerves and bones—wanted to tremble. Wordlessly, and with jerky movements, she scribbled down the items she wanted and thrust the pad and pen back at him.

He tore off the top sheet, glanced at it, then up at her, eyebrows raised. *"Needlepoint?"*

Lucia desperately wanted to shout at him, perhaps paraphrase her favorite line from her favorite Sandra Bullock movie: *Look, guy, I'm having a bad day. I've shot and maybe killed a man, and been threatened with death by a crazy woman, skinned my knees and lost a pair of very expensive shoes, and ruined an even more expensive designer gown. Don't* mess *with me!*

Instead, she met his gaze with steady calm and said, "I do needlepoint to relax. Otherwise my brain won't shut off. Okay?"

"Fascinating," Corbett murmured, eyelids at half-mast. "I would never have guessed."

"I guess you don't know me as well as you thought you did," Lucia snapped back, in no mood to be patronized.

The moment stretched…and stretched…long enough for it to come to her, what it was that was making her feel so unsettled. She was beginning to realize she didn't know Corbett Lazlo all that well, either.

Chapter 4

I've known her for more than ten years, Corbett thought. *I hired her, trained her, I've worked with her nearly every day of those ten years, and she's right. I don't really know her...do I?*

It was an unsettling thought, in the way earthquakes are unsettling. This one rocked the very foundations of his own convictions, shook his confidence in his own beliefs, made him wonder how much he really knew about anything—or at least about the people in his life.

But it was only the latest in the series of tremors that had shaken him tonight, shaken him to his very core.

I have a son.

A son, moreover, who was bent on killing him.

The boy's mother, the woman he'd once cared for, in his fashion, and long believed to be dead, was very much alive, and bent not only on killing him, but also on destroying everything in the world that mattered to him, including the woman he…loved.

Yes, God help me. Love. What other word could he use to express how much she meant to him?

And *that* woman, whom he had always considered to be someone in need of his protection, had saved *his* life tonight.

Under the circumstances, he thought he might be forgiven some slight discomposure.

What he really was, though he hated to admit it, was exhausted. Tonight he felt every one of his forty-eight years, and a few more besides. Awful thought: Was it possible that a man rounding the corner and homing in on the half-century mark might be getting too old for this business?

Rubbish. He'd be fine, he told himself, once he'd had a hot shower and a good night's sleep.

Though he suspected it was going to be a good long while before he could enjoy either of those things.

First, he had to get Lucia to a place beyond Cassandra's considerable reach. And there was only one place he knew of where he could be certain she would be safe. Besides himself, only Adam knew of its existence, and not even Adam knew exactly where it was located. Which meant the only way to get Lucia there was to take her himself.

Furthermore, after tonight's events he was reasonably certain the only way to ensure she would remain there, short of chaining her to the wall, would be to stay and personally see that she did.

He'd been through these facts in his mind again and again, trying to find another way, but it always came up the same: For the foreseeable future, he was going to have to live in close—one could say *intimate*—proximity to the woman he'd been trying desperately for the past ten years to maintain as much distance from as possible.

Bloody hypocrite. The voice of his conscience, which most of the time he was able to ignore—on this subject, at least—chided from the back row of his mind. *If you were really trying to avoid contact with the woman, you wouldn't keep challenging her to martial arts duels. And you didn't* really *have to take her with you to the embassy tonight...did you?*

Truthfully? Probably not. And if I hadn't done both of those things, I'd most likely be dead.

So. Nothing for it but to carry on, face the woman standing before him with her chin at a stubborn tilt and her cheeks flushed with anger. Face her and reply as he always did, with dignity and decorum, keeping the vivid memory of what her body felt like pinned beneath his, hot and moist with exertion, heart thumping, chest heaving against his, her woman's scent like a fog in his brain...keep all that buried in the deepest and most private reaches of his soul. As he always did.

He'd faced armed killers with less trepidation.

"Perhaps not." He answered her question in a voice carefully devoid of all expression, keeping his eyes veiled, as well. "Perhaps I don't know you at all. However, I think I can safely assume you might like to, uh...freshen up after our evening's adventures. While we wait for your belongings to arrive, I should imagine there's time for a shower, if you wish."

How stuffy he sounds—like a British schoolmaster.

Sorely tempted to tell him so, Lucia instead merely inclined her head formally and murmured, "Thank you. That would be nice."

After all the shocks that had rocked her this evening, the prospect of getting naked in Corbett Lazlo's bathroom barely registered on the Richter scale.

A sense of unreality enveloped her as she followed him through the tastefully decorated but impersonal living room, down a hallway past several intriguingly closed doors and into a large bedroom—his, obviously. Like the living room, it was furnished in a typically masculine style, but here at least were a few personal touches: A photograph of his parents—a snapshot taken on a windy day with a lake in the background; a dark blue robe tossed carelessly across the foot of a king-sized bed; an open book lying facedown on a table beside a comfortable chair, a pair of reading glasses perched crookedly atop the spine.

But the feature that immediately caught and held her attention was the huge domed skylight above the bed. She halted and stared up at it, captivated by the pale glow from the cloudy Paris night through rain-washed glass.

Corbett had crossed the room without pausing and now, with his hand on an ornate doorknob, turned to give her an inquiring look.

She glanced at him briefly, then went back to gazing at the subtle dance of light in the ceiling. "It must be amazing when there's something to see," she said lightly, for some reason reluctant to give away her true feelings. Particularly the wave of homesickness that had come over her so unexpectedly, sweeping her back to childhood camping trips in the California high country, happy times spent with her parents far away from the heartaches and pressures of being an overachieving misfit, too smart to fit in with the popular kids and too pretty to find acceptance among the geek crowd. She could almost smell the sun-warmed pines and crushed meadow grass, and the particular scent of her father's flannel shirt and lucky fishing vest. If she closed her eyes…

"Having come much too near to losing the privilege forever, I do like to be able to see the stars," Corbett said. His tone was dry, and his head tilted now at an angle that seemed almost defensive.

Lucia gave him a sideways look from under her lashes as she went to join him. "I never would have guessed," she said, mimicking his earlier remark to her.

He shot back, deadpan, "I guess you don't know *me* as well as you thought."

It was too close to her own musings, and she didn't reply.

He gave the knob a turn, opening a door in the wood paneling into what turned out to be a dressing room and closet, though it was larger than the bedroom in Lucia's tiny two-room apartment on the other side of the river. From a bank of shelves he took a folded bathrobe, snowy white, the thick, plush kind found in very expensive hotels. She wondered if he kept a supply handy for all his female guests. She wondered—but only briefly—if any of those guests ever shared the shower with their host. *Or that view of the stars.*

"The bathroom is through there. You will find clean towels in the linen cupboard next to the fireplace—" *fireplace?* "—and, uh…anything else you might need, shampoo and whatnot, are in the chest of drawers nearest the window."

"Thank you," Lucia murmured, carefully avoiding eye contact. She thought again, *He sounds like a well-trained butler.*

All at once she felt vulnerable. And even more incomprehensible, as she discovered when she was standing naked under the pounding deluge of deliciously hot shower spray, she felt a pressing need to cry.

It was a delayed reaction to having shot and almost killed someone and having herself been threatened with death, she tried to tell herself. Because that would at least be understandable. She might even reasonably allow herself to give in to it.

And she might have done so, except she knew that wasn't what was making her feel like this. She knew, because she'd felt exactly like this once before, almost ten years ago, when her life had taken an irrevocable turn. And she'd known even then that there would be no going back. That nothing would ever be the same again….

He was the first thing she saw when she walked into the student center, a tall, slender, dark-haired man wearing a beautifully tailored dark suit. She noticed him even in the huge arena crowded with eager job-seeking students and the elaborate displays of prospective employers hoping to recruit the best of the best, noticed him because of his natural elegance, and because he didn't seem to belong to any particular company, and because, even in that noisy and brightly lit place, something about him struck her as mysterious, enigmatic. Like a man accustomed to living in the shadows.

Maybe the CIA, she thought, intrigued. *They would be recruiting here, as would the FBI. Or, maybe, one of the even more secretive agencies, the ones that aren't supposed to exist.*

"Who do you suppose that is?" she asked her companion, Ricky Choy, who, being five-feet-two, gay and completely obsessed at the time with artificial intelligence, was one of the few people she felt comfortable enough with to call friend.

Ricky had bobbed up onto his tiptoes and was craning his neck in a futile effort to see over the milling crowd. Bobbing back down again, he shrugged and said, "Why don't you go ask him?" He was giving his backpack nervous hitches, clearly eager to be off. "I'm gonna go check out Dreamforce. Rumor is, they've got a new A.I. project that's going to knock the competition out of the water. Man, if I could get—"

"Go," she said, waving him off. Then she added with a sly look and a grin, "Gonna stop by and see what B.G. has to offer?"

Ricky gave an "As if!" eyeroll. Like most techies, he had a love/hate relationship with the giant Microsoft. A moment later he had disappeared into the crowd.

She took a deep breath, shifted her own backpack onto one shoulder and was about to move off in the other direction when something…an odd compulsion…made her turn and look once more at the man in the dark suit. And for some reason—an odd coincidence?—found him looking straight back at her. For a moment, before they moved on, his eyes locked with hers, and in that moment she felt a shiver run down her spine.

Why not?

She threaded her way through the shifting crowd toward the dark-haired man. Shadow man, *she thought.*

His gaze followed her progress until she stood directly in front of him. His eyes were anything but shadowed. Instead, they were a light but curiously intense shade of blue, the color of polished steel.

"Are you recruiting?" she daringly asked him, in the half defensive, half belligerent way she was accustomed to addressing attractive strangers.

"Maybe," he replied. His gaze made her intensely self-conscious, though not in the usual way. "What's your field?"

"Computer science."

He nodded, and his gaze didn't waver. "Are you job-hunting?"

"Maybe." She looked at him sideways. "I haven't decided. I might go to grad school instead. So...what company are you with?"

Instead of answering, he produced a business card. She took it, glanced at it, then looked up at him, still wary, but feeling the deep-down buzz of interest. "The Lazlo Group. I've never heard of it."

He smiled, very slightly. "I should be quite surprised if you had." He had a pronounced British accent, which only added to the air of mystery that seemed to hang about him like a signature scent.

"And you would be—" frowning up at him, she tapped the card with a fingertip "—Corbett Lazlo?"

His head made an elegant dip. "I am."

"There's no phone number or e-mail address on this card. Where would I send my résumé? I mean, if I do decide to apply for a job with you?"

His eyes were veiled now, the little smile more self-confident than arrogant. "I already know what I need to know about you...Lucia Cordez. As for your job qualifications, if you succeed in finding me, that's all the résumé you need."

He inclined his head briefly and turned away, leaving her momentarily speechless. She recovered enough wit to call after him, "Yes, but...wait. How do you know I even want—" —to work for you!

But he had already vanished into the crowd.

"Interesting approach," Ricky remarked from somewhere near her elbow. "As gorgeous as he is, I bet he's a bitch to work for."

"What makes you think I'd want to?" she snapped back, taking her anger out on him because she was infuriated by the chorus of voices inside her head singing, "Oh, but I do, I do!"

Two days later, she stared at a terse e-mail message on her computer screen:

Well done, Lucia. You found me in less than 48 hours. Are you ready to take the next step?

Hands poised above the keyboard, poised to tell Corbett Lazlo what he could do with his job, she felt strange shivers inside, a peculiar lurch in her midsection, the rapid beating of her pulse, fully aware that a single word would send her life hurtling off in a new and exciting—perhaps frightening—direction.

Her hands trembled a little as she typed the only word necessary:

Yes.

* * *

It hadn't been that simple, of course. That had been only the beginning of Corbett Lazlo's courtship of her—there really was no better word for it. And once he'd won her commitment to work for him, he'd begun to transform her from shy duckling to confident swan. From awkward college student to sophisticated world traveler, equally comfortable conversing with kings or camel drivers. From computer geek to resident techno-genius for the most elite private-security agency in the world.

She'd become a sophisticate, a technowiz, true...one with the skills, training and nerve to kill.

Lucia turned off the hot water with an impatient jerk and stood for a moment with her eyes closed, breathing evenly through her nostrils, angry with herself. And ashamed.

She'd chosen the Lazlo Group as much as it—or *he*—had chosen her. And tonight she'd saved Corbett's life.

She couldn't even let herself think about what her life would be like without him. She owed Corbett Lazlo everything. He'd taught her to believe in herself, to value herself as a whole woman, rather than hate what she'd always seen as an awkward bunch of mismatched parts. He'd taught her how to protect herself in a dangerous world, and shown her parts of that world she'd never known existed. It wasn't his fault she'd fallen in love with him almost from the first moment she'd laid eyes on him.

Quit fussing, she scolded herself. So she had to go to a safe house? Half the agents in the Group were hiding out in safe houses at the moment. The entire agency was in crisis, fighting for its very life. Time for her to step up, put her skills to work and do everything in her power to help save it.

But now the thought nagged at her: *If only I'd been able to track the source of those e-mails! If I'd been able to find out who was sending them, all this might not have happened.*

And a young man, Corbett's son, might not be fighting for his life in a Paris hospital.

Resolved, grounded and considerably refreshed, she stepped from the shower onto a thick plush rug that was warm from the gas log fire in the Italian-tile fireplace nearby. Picking up an equally toasty towel, she dried her hair, then her body, wincing a bit when the soft Egyptian cotton grazed over the skinned places on her legs and elbows. She slipped into the snowy white robe, then leaned close to the mirror to inspect her normally even, café-au-lait complexion, though her cheeks were more dusky rose now from the heat of the shower, and her nose and forehead glistened with a fine sheen of moisture. Odd, she thought, how such incredible things can happen, things that change everything, even who we are, and yet nothing shows.

My face is the same…exactly the same. And yet, I feel as though I'm looking at the face of a stranger.

Shaking off a small residual chill, she combed her fingers through the damp tangle of her curls, gave the robe's belt tie a final tug and opened the bathroom door.

And felt all her newly built buttresses crumbling like gingerbread in the rain.

"I'm sorry," Corbett said, his voice diffident to the point of gruffness. "I'm afraid I'm going to have to ask for your help."

He was standing in the dressing-room doorway, dressed only in a pair of black cargo pants, his body outlined in the rich red-gold textures of the bedroom behind him. One hand was braced on the doorframe; the other he held tightly across his ribs, as if, at that moment, it was the only thing keeping his torso from breaking apart. At his feet lay a pile of elastic bandage, half of it still neatly rolled. The other end originated somewhere in the coils that had fallen loosely about his waist.

"I can see that." The words were from her own throat but came so calmly, so easily they seemed to have been spoken by someone else. As she moved toward him she was enveloped in the heady blend of scents peculiar to a fastidious, well-groomed man: leather and lamb's wool, Bay Rum and cedar, a trace of expensive pipe tobacco. She hadn't noticed it before, but now it seemed exotic and at the same time oddly familiar. Almost dizzy with it, she bent to gather up the pile of unwound bandage from the floor.

"Dropped the damn thing." Corbett's voice rumbled above her, muted and angry. "Can't seem to bend over. These ribs…"

"Maybe you shouldn't have dashed out of the hospital before they had a chance to patch you up." She straightened, aware of the heat in her cheeks and glad to have a legitimate reason for it. "Your ribs are probably broken—cracked, at least."

"We were in a bit of a hurry," he snapped back at her. "As I recall. And there's not much they could have done in any case. Nothing I can't do myself just as well. Here, give me that."

She held the roll of bandage away from him as he reached for it. "Oh, yeah, I can see you're doing a bang-up job." She kept her eyes on her hands, watched them rapidly roll up the unwound pile of bandage. When she'd run out of slack and the taut bandage was a short tether between them, she lifted her eyes and forced them to meet his. And found them sharp as frost crystals. Her heartbeat was hard and fast. She took a breath. "Hold out your arms."

This is intolerable, Corbett thought, as he reluctantly obeyed. He knew from personal experience that there were worse tortures, but at the moment couldn't seem to think of one. His heart was thumping against his injured ribs, and even that small assault was painful.

He knew she was right. She could do the job better and, what was more important right now, faster than he could. But how in bloody hell could he stand having her so near, for as long as it would take her to bind up his ribs, when she was warm from the shower and smelled so sweet, and he could almost taste the dew on her skin.

"All right, but do it tightly," he said, holding himself ramrod straight and grinding the words between his teeth. "It's got to be tight enough to keep my chest from expanding when I breathe."

She gave him a withering glance. "That's totally wrong, you know. You have to be able to breathe, even if it hurts. And when you breathe, your chest expands— even I know that much."

He rolled his eyes, then glared at her. "Must you argue about this? It's only for the trip—it's likely to jostle a bit, and I'd just as soon not have to deal with the humiliating possibility that I might pass out from the pain. Do you mind?"

"Oh, all right," she grumbled, glaring back at him. "You know, it would really help if you could relax. Here, hold this."

He took the end of the bandage from her and clamped it snugly against his left pectoral, just above his wildly thumping heart, like someone pledging undying fealty. He set his jaw and stared fixedly over her tangle of fragrant curls with his face frozen in what he hoped was an expression of heroic stoicism.

Ignoring his efforts, Lucia drew the bandage in a diagonal line across his chest, ducked under his extended arm and moved behind him. And only then did he allow his eyes to close.

Some dark angel inside him couldn't resist needling her. "That's not going to be tight enough."

She snarled back at him. "I'm just getting it started—do you mind? Just...stop trying to boss me, okay? You're not my teacher anymore."

The silence which followed that declaration—startled, on his part, and judging from the set of her mouth and chin when she glared at him around his shoulder, wounded on hers—stretched between them until it became excruciating. And all that time her words careened and ricocheted wildly inside his head, setting off little explosions of enlightenment wherever they struck.

I'm not *her teacher.*
She's a grown woman.
I've been treating her like a child.
No wonder she's angry.

I owe her my life.

What did she mean *by that?*

Dear God, how angry is she?

His stomach did a curious little flip-flop he hated to acknowledge was fear.

"What on earth possessed you?" She was squarely in front of him again, her gaze fixed on the center of his chest, each cheek sporting a bright spot of pink. "To let him get so close? What if he'd shot you in the neck, or your face?" Her eyes lifted and flashed at him, diamond bright with fury. "Did you even *think* about that?"

Forgetting he couldn't, Corbett tried to draw a deep breath. He hissed shallowly, then pressed his lips together and waited until he had control of the pain again. Because he knew she was right, he tried his best to explain what was inexplicable. But how could he explain what had made him hesitate when he didn't know himself?

"I didn't want to spook him, I suppose," he said tightly. "Afraid he might blow the attempt again…try to run for it. I wanted to take him alive."

And he could have kicked himself for the last sentence when she looked up at him and he saw the bleakness, the stark fear in her eyes. His tired mind cast about for words that wouldn't make her feel worse than she already did, but he rejected them all as platitudes. Meaningless clichés. The one thing he thought of doing that might conceivably ease her heart and mind, he also rejected. Because he hadn't the right. She was dead on about his not being her teacher anymore, but he wasn't her lover, either. He wasn't even her friend, not really, even though he cared for her. A lot. But he had no right to take her in his arms. No right to hold her against his heart, stroke her hair, kiss her tear-damp eyelids, whisper reassurances against her lips before he kissed them, too.

No, he had no right.

But, oh, how I want to.

"And…you had no idea he was your son?" she asked it in a hesitant whisper.

Overwhelmed by his thoughts, he could only shake his head.

"Corbett, I'm so sorry—I didn't mean to shoot him. If I could have hit him harder—disabled him—maybe he wouldn't have been able to go for the gun…"

He couldn't stand it. He clutched her by the arms, and the remaining roll of bandage fell once more to the floor. Her anguished eyes stared up at him as words grated harshly from between his tightly clenched teeth.

"Stop it. Just…stop it right now. You did what you were trained to do. What *I* trained you to do. You did what you had to do to save another agent's life. *My* life…as it happens." His attempt at a smile was a miserable failure.

Her gaze didn't waver. "The fact remains," she said softly, "I shot your son. I may have killed him. He could still die, Corbett. And I will be the one who killed him. How could you ever forgive me for that?"

He couldn't answer her. Shaken to his very core, Corbett finally did the thing he'd told himself he could not do. Must not do. He touched her lips with his finger to silence her, then with great care and gentleness, folded her into his arms.

Carefully…gently…not because of the pain of his fractured ribs—he no longer felt that—but because his need to hold her was so fierce, so intense, so terrible it frightened him.

And that was something he couldn't let her, or anyone, know.

Chapter 5

Time passed. Lucia had no idea how much, only that she willed this moment to go on and on, knowing the sharp, bright stab of happiness was too intense to live beyond that…a single moment, knowing whatever powerful emotion had moved Corbett to embrace her would pass, and that when it did the joy inside her would turn to equally intense pain.

And so her reasoning mind bolted for cover like a terrified bunny huddled in darkness, believing it meant safety, while her tired body snuggled into the dangerous haven of his arms.

"Lucia…" His breath sighed unevenly through her hair, and she felt his fingers there, too.

No thinking…no thinking…

Wonder lay on her like soft wool as she lifted her face to the warm hollow of his neck and shoulder. She felt the beat of his pulse on her lips, felt his heart thump against the thick bandage wrap that lay between his chest and hers. She felt the textures of the bandage with her palms, and…when had she put her arms around him? She felt his hand on her back, moving slowly downward to her waist, then below, felt the pressure, subtle at first, then more insistent, pressing her closer… closer.

Someone was shaking. Was it her? Was it him? Panic lurked. A whimper threatened.

No thinking!

Obeying only that directive and stubbornly blind to all consequences, she moved her head, brushing her lips over his skin, savoring the feel of it, the warmth and smoothness, then the roughness of beard, the hard ridge of jaw. She heard his breath catch, then stop. She held hers…and his mouth came searching. Her lips parted, and his breath flowed gently over them. She held herself still….

In the stillness they both heard it: the rhythmic thumping, too firm and steady to mistake for their galloping heartbeats.

Lucia's eyes flew open in time to see the helicopter's shadow flit across the skylight. She felt Corbett's body stiffen. He lifted his head and his hands came gently but firmly to grip her shoulders and hold her away from him.

"Sounds like our ride has arrived," he said, and his voice had a ragged edge she'd never heard before. Just for an instant his eyes burned into hers, before she nodded and stepped back, fingers pressed to her lips, trapping the tiniest of whimpers behind them.

"I've left some clothes for you—here on the dressing table. They'll be too big—especially the boots, but they'll keep your feet warm. Put on both pairs of socks—that should help." As he spoke, he was reeling in the trailing end of bandage.

She took it from him, carefully avoiding his eyes while she brought the end of the bandage to the one just below his collarbone, tied and pulled the knot tight and tucked in the ends. "My things…"

"Yes, of course. I imagine you'll find them on board before you."

She lifted her eyes in an unspoken question, but they got no farther than his mouth, captivated by the lips that a moment ago had been a breath away from kissing hers. Now they seemed like the perfectly sculpted lips of a classical statue. That they moved when he spoke seemed magical to her.

"It's quite likely Adam ordered the chopper diverted to your flat, as backup in case of unexpected… developments."

She nodded. He touched her arm and turned to go, then hesitated. She held her breath, but at that moment from the bedroom came the polite trill of a telephone. He said, "Quickly…please." Then went out, closing the dressing-room door behind him.

Alone, enveloped in the scent that was so evocative of him it made her ache, Lucia let her defenses crumble. Eyes closed, she groped for something solid to hold on to and found the dressing table…gripped it and leaned on her hands while the shudders raced through her body, responses to emotions too overwhelming even for tears.

Don't think. Don't feel.

Since she was too tired to do either, she opened her eyes and found the neat pile of clothing Corbett had laid out for her: Black knit pants, ivory wool turtleneck pullover, black-and-ivory ski jacket. Après-ski boots and two pairs of soft, ultrawarm socks. Thermal-lined gloves, and even a black woolen cap to keep her ears warm. He'd thought of everything.

A small hiccup of laughter burst from her as she picked up the cap and touched it to her lips, then slipped it over her head and her still-damp hair and carefully adjusted it to cover her ears.

"Hello, Edward," Corbett said, cradling the phone awkwardly between jaw and shoulder while he picked up the pullover he'd laid out on the bed.

"Good gad, Corb, I just heard. Are you all right? What the devil's going on? They said you'd been *shot?*"

"Yes, well, good luck I was wearing body armor, eh?" Corbett's grin was wry. He pressed the speaker button and put the phone down on the bed, then pulled the shirt over his head. As he eased it over his bandaged ribs, he could hear his brother's snort of vexation.

"Luck? Don't tell me you were expecting something of the sort? And you let Lucia—"

"Precautions were taken," Corbett said patiently, slipping automatically into the placating manner he'd employed with his elder brother since childhood. "Lucia's fine. I'm fine. Everyone's fine."

"Yes, well, Mum's quite beside herself. Even Apu has been showing signs of concern, if you can imagine it. You might give them a ring, you know."

"Can't do it now, I'm afraid. I've a chopper waiting.

Do me a favor, won't you, and let them know I'm quite all right, occupational hazard, et cetera…"

"Off again, are you? I don't s'pose you care to let your next of kin in on where you're going and when you expect to return?"

"Sorry," Corbett said, mentally rolling his eyes at the petulance in his brother's tone, "you know the drill—client privilege and all that." Though he could and often did lie to his brother without a second thought, he didn't enjoy doing so. He told himself it wasn't that he didn't trust Edward—he did, as much as he trusted anyone. It was just that he was a firm believer in the old adage that the best way to keep one's secrets was to *keep* them—to oneself, that is.

"Must be off. I'll be in touch." He thumb-clicked the off button, cutting off whatever protests Edward was preparing to make.

Adam crossed the helipad at a jog to where Corbett waited in the wash from the chopper's rotors, shoulders hunched against the cold, hands thrust deep into pockets of his long overcoat. He withdrew them to clasp Adam's firmly in both of his and leaned closer to make himself heard about the noise. "How did it go?"

Adam hitched a shoulder and grinned. "Right as rain, mate."

"No trouble, then?"

"Nothing me and the boys couldn't handle."

"Ah," Corbett said, nodding absently.

"Just got word from the airfield. Citation's juiced up and waiting for you."

"Good. You cleared us for Salzburg?"

"Yep. You're good to go. As soon as—"

Both men turned together as, right on cue, the elevator door slid open. Adam wondered how being gutshot would compare to the twisting pain he felt in his belly, watching Lucia step out of that elevator and come toward them. Her eyes went straight to Corbett's and his stuck to her like limpets. This was it, the beginning of the end. Adam was about to put the two people he loved most in the world on a chopper and send them off to a private hideaway together. He guessed the odds they wouldn't figure out they were crazy in love with each other at slim to none.

He locked his grin in place and braced himself for Lucia's goodbye hug. "You behave yourself, you hear me? And no worries…"

"No worries," she answered back, with a little break. Then she kissed his cheek and ran for the waiting chopper, holding on to her hair with one hand.

Corbett was there again, gripping his hand hard. "Listen, my friend, you keep your head down. And watch your back. You know this is going to get ugly…"

"You can count on it."

Corbett paused, nodded and started to turn, but Adam caught his shoulder and held on.

"Just one thing." He wasn't smiling now, not even close, and he had to push his words past the rocks in his chest. "You know I love you like my own brother, but if you let anything happen to that lady, I will hunt you down like a dog."

For a long scary moment the other man's eyes burned into his. Then one corner of his mouth lifted. "You'll have to hunt me down in hell, then, brother, because if anything does happen to her, it'll be over my dead body."

"Right you are, then," Adam returned. "Just so we understand each other." He squeezed Corbett's shoulder and stepped back.

"I believe we do." Corbett gave him a little salute. "*Bonne chance,* old friend."

"G'day and good journey, mate."

He watched Corbett walk stiffly to the waiting helicopter and climb aboard then pull the door shut after him. Watched the shiny black LG chopper lift off, bank sharply and thunder away across the rooftops of the city. Unaware of the cold damp wind, he went on watching the chopper until it was just another pinprick of light in the clearing sky.

Someone was singing.

Lucia lay with her eyes closed and listened, enveloped in the luxurious warmth of a feather bed, the old-fashioned kind so soft and deep it seemed one might sink into it far enough to drop out of the world completely.

She'd certainly tried her best to do so last night, and for a time, it appeared, had succeeded. Her recollection of the last few hours of the journey, including the arrival at their destination, was limited to disconnected bits and pieces, a montage of hazy impressions:

Cold. Cold that stung her nose and cheeks and made her shiver even in the warm clothes she was wearing.

Fighting to stay awake, fighting a desire to sleep so overpowering it was like torture.

Moving, constantly moving—by helicopter to the

group's private airfield in the French countryside not far from Paris, then by private jet to Salzburg, and finally, by rented car through Austria and into Hungary—so that even when the motion stopped, her body still felt as if she were in a boat on a choppy sea.

Delighted greetings delivered in hushed voices, in a language she recognized only enough to identify as Hungarian.

Warm soup, pungent with garlic and paprika. Gentle hands leading her, guiding her, helping her undress. And into bed. And the sensation of falling into a warm and welcoming darkness.

Where she lay now, listening to the sounds of dishes clattering and cookware clanking and someone singing.

It wasn't a radio or television or CD player. The voice was female, untrained and probably not young, but had a joyous lack of self-awareness that made it captivating in spite of a tendency to crack and warble. And even though Hungarian wasn't one of the languages in which Lucia was fluent, and she could only understand a word here and there, the tune was so catchy, the rhythm so bouncy, it made her smile.

She opened her eyes to gray daylight that seemed to come from a small round skylight in the center of the room. There were no windows. There would not be in a house, as Corbett had told her, that was mostly underground. She drew her arms from under the downy comforter and, stretching, bumped one elbow against an embroidered wall hanging. The bed was roughly twin-sized and daybed style, with one long side against the wall. The embroidery was thick and lush, intricate patterns of stylized birds and flowers done in vivid colors on felt backing. Having tried her hand at embroidery, as well as cross-stitch and needlepoint, Lucia knew true artistry when she saw it.

Intriguing aromas—coffee and others less familiar—were beginning to drift into the room along with the singing, and Lucia's stomach gave an enthusiastic response. Last night's bowl of soup had been both warm and filling, but was now only a dim memory. She was, she realized, famished.

Throwing back the comforter, she wallowed up out of the feather bed and in doing so made several discoveries that nurtured the amazingly upbeat mood with which she'd awakened. For one thing, she was wearing a loose nightshirt made of thin, much-washed cotton that felt soft as a caress on her skin. And the rug beneath her bare feet was warm sheepskin.

When had she become so aware of these purely sensual things?

How odd it was to feel such a sense of well-being after the last forty-eight nightmarish hours.

The room was fairly large, and it needed to be in order to accommodate the several massive pieces of furniture, which in addition to the bed included a wardrobe, chest and dresser, all carved and painted with flowers and birds in the same style as the embroidery. Looking around, she discovered two more causes for rejoicing: The bags Adam had packed for her, and which she hadn't yet had a chance to explore, had been brought in and were waiting for her on a low chest near the foot of the bed. And she had a private bathroom—tiny, but complete with a bathtub and a handheld shower nozzle!

As safe houses went, she thought, this one could probably be considered downright luxurious.

The bouncy little tune now seemed to be permanently stuck in her mind, and she hummed it while she set about discovering what sorts of personal belongings Adam had considered essential for a woman in protective exile. Her personal laptop, of course; that one was a no-brainer. And, yes, the floppy handwoven cloth bag containing her current needlepoint projects and supplies. Her overnighter, she found, held toiletries, cosmetics, makeup and…yes, underwear. She couldn't help it—her cheeks burned as she explored the selection and realized just *how* thorough Adam had been.

In her big roll-along suitcase she found not only the clothes she'd probably have chosen if she'd packed for herself, but other things, thoughtful little things, some even she might not have thought of. The framed photograph of her parents and her alarm clock from her nightstand; her MP3 player; the glasses she wore when her eyes got tired, and out of sheer vanity, only at home; her digital camera; the novel she'd been reading with her place still marked; the battery-free LCD flashlight from her nightstand drawer—her section of Paris was prone to power outages; the little tin of her favorite hard candies.

The happy little song died on her lips as she held the pretty tin and thought of Adam with wistful sadness. If only she could be in love with *him,* she thought, instead of Corbett, who only saw her as his protégée. Though, of course, she *did* love Adam. She loved him dearly, but unfortunately for both of them, rather like the brother she'd never had.

And thinking of Corbett…

He was here somewhere. Close by. Perhaps even now he was sitting in that aromatic kitchen, drinking coffee, smiling along with the singer. For the next several days—who knew how long?—she'd be sharing his living quarters, his personal space. Would he finally let her begin to know him, not just as employer but as a person…a man? Especially after those precious moments in his apartment.

Would he have kissed her if the helicopter hadn't interrupted? A knot gathered in her chest, and a little shiver rippled through her.

Hurrying, she selected a pair of jeans and a pullover sweater in rich coppery tones she knew complemented her hair and skin, picked up her overnighter and went into the bathroom. The thought of a hot bath was a seductive one, but she was even more eager to be out and about. To go…to see…

Corbett. His face filled her mind, his eyes burned into her memory. She could almost feel his hand on her back, sliding low…pressing her close. Could almost smell his skin…taste it.

Ruthlessly shaking off the memories, she washed quickly, noting as she did that the bathroom, like the adjacent bedroom, was cool but not frigid, in spite of there being no evidence of a heater anywhere. Another aspect of being underground, she imagined. Most likely it would stay evenly cool year round.

Deciding her hair was a wild tangle that she lacked the patience to deal with this morning, she caught it into a gold clasp at the nape of her neck and finger-curled the few tendrils that had managed to escape capture, so that they fell naturally against her cheeks and temples.

Then, heart quickening, she composed herself and opened the bedroom door.

And found herself in a large, bright kitchen, which, to her chagrin, was empty except for the woman busily rolling out pastry dough on the flour-covered table. Obviously the singer—she was still humming the jaunty little tune. Evidently, it was firmly stuck in her mind, too.

She broke it off and turned at the sound of the opening door. In spite of a dandelion fluff of snow-white hair, her face was young, unlined except for smile creases at the corners of her eyes and mouth. She was quite short, and plump in an appealing way, so well-endowed both fore and aft that she reminded Lucia of a little white hen. Her skin was sprinkled with light brown freckles, and her eyes were a clear, vivid blue. Corbett's eyes.

Seeing Lucia, her flushed face blossomed with a smile, and she gave a little cry that was both a delighted welcome and dismay at her own floury, disheveled state. Hurriedly brushing her hands on her apron and chattering too rapidly for Lucia to understand, she became a small whirlwind of activity, somehow managing to guide Lucia to the far end of the table while almost simultaneously, it seemed, providing her with plate, utensils, napkin and a cup of steaming hot coffee. Lucia barely had time to note that both the napkin and table-cloth were snowy white and decorated with the same exquisite embroidery as the wall hangings in her room, before platters heaped with cold meats, fresh rolls, hard-boiled eggs and assorted pickled vegetables and fruit preserves appeared before her.

At the same time she was flitting about the kitchen, the woman kept up a rapid-fire chatter that didn't seem to require a reply. Lucia kept smiling and nodding and saying the words, *Köszönöm szépen,* which she knew meant, *thank you very much.* And when, during a pause in the other woman's monologue, she managed to insert the Hungarian words for *milk* and *sugar,* the woman clapped her hands like a delighted child.

Having produced a pitcher of milk and a small bowl of sugar, the woman paused, pulled out a chair and seated herself on its edge, like a hen on her perch. Then, speaking slowly and carefully, she asked—in Hungarian—if Lucia spoke *magyarul.* And she had an odd way of pronouncing her name, making it "*Lee-sia,*" rather than Lu-*see*-a.

Lucia shook her head apologetically. "Only a little."

The woman merely smiled even wider and made an erasing motion with her hands as if to say, no problem. Then, speaking slowly and with much use of gestures, she introduced herself as Kati and asked if Lucia had slept well.

Once again Lucia was able to produce the right words from her tiny vocabulary. *"Nagyon jól, köszönöm."* She was less successful, however, when she tried to ask about Corbett.

Kati seemed confused until Lucia tried asking instead about "Mr. Lazlo." This time she got a bright smile, a nod and an enthusiastic, "Ah, *Lacsi!*"

From there she went happily into explanations, apparently having forgotten Lucia's language limitations, until interrupted by some thumps and scufflings from outside the door. At this she popped out of the chair, clutching her apron, and began to bustle about, setting another place at the table.

Lucia sipped coffee and fought to compose herself while her heart lurched into overdrive.

The door opened and a man entered the kitchen along with a swirl of cool damp air. Corbett, of course. Yes, but a Corbett so different from the one Lucia knew, if Kati had introduced him to her as some other Lazlo— a long-lost brother or cousin, perhaps—she would not have been surprised.

He was wearing a fur hat, dark wool trousers tucked into high boots, a heavy coat that hung open to show its sheepskin lining and a laced-up vest over a dark green shirt. In the crook of one arm he carried a rifle—not the first time Lucia had seen him with a weapon in his hands, of course, but this time Corbett seemed at once less lethal and more…stalwart. Masculine. Though, that may have been partly because he was also unshaven, the dark stubble and cold-reddened cheeks making his eyes seem even bluer than they usually were.

I can't stare, Lucia thought, and quickly looked away. *My eyes…my face will surely give me away.*

But Corbett barely glanced at her, his eyes flicking over her as he nodded a mute good-morning.

Lucia watched silently from the corner of her eye as he put the rifle on brackets above the door then turned to greet Kati with a wide smile, bending down so she could kiss him soundly on both cheeks. This activity left him liberally dusted with flour, which Kati tried to brush off his vest, only making matters worse.

Sadness, a kind of wistful envy, caught at Lucia's throat as she watched the two of them laughing and bantering back and forth with what was obviously easy familiarity and genuine affection. It spread through her chest like a strangling vine, when Corbett, having shed his coat and hat, seated himself at the table and faced her at last, and she watched the robust stranger vanish in a heartbeat, along with the smile.

"Did you sleep well?" The question and tone were formal, proper, correct. Corbett as usual.

The well-trained butler was back, Lucia thought as she replied, "Yes, thank you for asking," determined not to be outdone in the matter of manners, at least. She picked up her coffee cup and sipped without tasting.

"I see you've met Katalin."

"Yes, though the introductions just about covered the extent of my Hungarian." She smiled and raised her cup to Kati, who was standing behind Corbett, beaming at the two of them, floury hands wrapped in her apron.

"Ah. Perhaps I should tell you, Kati can speak English," he said dryly. "She just prefers not to."

Upon hearing this, Kati made a hideous face at Corbett's back, and Lucia ducked her head and drank more coffee to hide a smile and a quivery gulp of laughter.

After a moment she set down her cup and steeling herself, lifted her eyes to his face. He wasn't looking at her, of course. He hadn't, not really, not directly in the eyes, since the encounter in his dressing room. When he'd come so close to kissing her. So this was how it was going to be from now on?

Damn you, no!

Clamping her teeth together, she counted slowly to five, then asked bluntly, "And how are your ribs this morning? Were *you* able to get any sleep?"

He grunted and made a brushing motion with his hand, dismissing both the question and his injury as of no consequence. So much, she thought, for good manners.

Silence fell, except for Kati, who had gone back to her pastry and was once again humming the catchy Hungarian tune. The room was sultry and fragrant with cooking smells. Warm. Cozy. Comfortable. Or it should have been.

The silence became too much for Corbett. The twin spots of color on Lucia's cheeks shamed him. The images in his mind tormented him—her eyes, bright with angry tears as she'd said the words he'd been hearing ever since, even in his sleep.

"You're not my teacher anymore...."

But what had happened—*almost* happened—between them was in no way even remotely her fault. He was behaving like a first-class jackass.

Taking up his coffee cup, and along with it his lagging self-control, he produced what he hoped was a pleasant expression and directed it at the object of his tortured thoughts.

"So," he said, "what do you think of my hideaway?"

She gave him a sideways glance as she attacked a chunk of *kolbász* with her knife and fork—obviously angry with him still. "I haven't seen much of it, except for my room and this one."

"Well, then, you've seen most of it. Other than that, there's just my study. There." He gestured with his cup toward one of the two doors that opened off the back of the kitchen.

She paused with a bit of sausage halfway to her mouth to look at him with eyebrows raised. "Then...

I've taken your bedroom?" She put down her knife and fork, her lips tightening. "You shouldn't have done that. I can just as well sleep in the study."

"Actually, you can't," Corbett said, spearing a slice of ham with his fork and bringing it to his mouth. "I'll show you around in a bit, if you'd like. After we've done as much damage to this excellent repast as we possibly can. Kati will never forgive us if we don't."

He looked at his old friend in time to catch her putting her tongue out at him, gave her a smile in return, then glanced at Lucia and found her staring fixedly at her plate, as though she was about to burst into tears.

What the bloody hell did I say now? Resigned to the fact that he was never going to be able to understand the woman, he stabbed at a pickled pepper and made no further attempt at conversation for the remainder of the meal.

Though she had no appetite, Lucia managed to eat a roll and a piece of the spicy, hard Hungarian sausage, as well as some peach compote that was really quite delicious. Resisting Kati's urging to eat more, she excused herself and went to the bedroom, where she tidied the bed, brushed her teeth, then packed all her things back into her suitcases. She was determined not to put Corbett out of his own bed for one more night.

She gave her face a critical once-over in the bathroom mirror, decided against lipstick, then took a fortifying breath and went back to the kitchen, where she found Corbett leaning against the sink and chatting quietly with Kati, evidently waiting for her.

When Lucia entered, he straightened and turned to

put his cup in the sink, then placed one hand on Kati's shoulder and said something to her in Hungarian, too low and rapid for Lucia to catch.

He turned to her, his expression relaxed and pleasant but completely impersonal, reminding her that she was an employee and temporary guest, nothing more. "Ready for the grand tour?"

"Absolutely. Will I need a jacket?"

"For the moment, no. We'll do the indoor bit first. Shall we?" He waved her toward the far end of the kitchen, opposite the door he'd come in through and to the left of the bedroom. "First, this is the pantry—or storeroom, actually." He reached past her to open the door on the right and gestured for her to precede him.

As she stepped through the door she saw only blackness. Then bright light flooded the area around her as Corbett reached past her to flip on the switch. Beyond the light the darkness thinned to gray, and she could see that they were not in a room at all, but in the cave itself. The air was cool, and in spite of the quiet hum of ventilation fans, she could detect a faint odor of sulfur.

"Don't mind the smell," Corbett said, as if he'd read her mind. "There are thermal springs back in there. That's where we get our hot water. I meant to warn you— we do filter the water, but you might still notice the sulfur smell. Don't worry—the cold water, for drinking and cooking and such, comes from a well outside."

"You've certainly made good use of your natural resources," Lucia murmured, gazing around at the shelves and boxes filled with provisions. "Are those fans the only ventilation? I feel a breeze."

"Oh, no. The fans merely augment the natural airflow. There's a sort of chimney back in there, you see. Comes out in the castle ruins on top of the hill."

"There's a *castle?* Really?" She turned to him, her anger with him forgotten, for the moment. "Is it yours? Can I see it?"

His smile flickered like a faulty lightbulb; his eyes touched her, then looked away. "Yes, of course. Though it's nothing but a ruin now, I'm afraid. In medieval times, the castle's defenders used the chimney and the cave as an escape route, and as a secret means to bring in water and supplies during a siege. They carved steps and handholds that are still there, although I don't imagine anyone's used them for a good many years."

Lucia would like to have asked to see the secret escape route—certainly she'd have asked many more questions. But she could see Corbett was impatient to get on with the tour, so she merely murmured, "Fascinating," and followed him back to the kitchen.

"And this," he said, closing one door and opening the other, "is my…study—for want of a better word."

Acutely conscious of the person whose private space she was about to enter, Lucia peered hesitantly over his outstretched arm. Then, with an awed, "Oh, my goodness…" she advanced past him and into the room.

The room was smaller than the bedroom, well-ventilated and, when Corbett flipped a switch, brightly lit. And almost every square foot of space was taken up with state-of-the-art computers and the very latest in communications equipment.

She whirled back to Corbett, a dozen questions poised on the tip of her tongue. One side of his mouth tilted upward in a sardonic little smile.

"So I trust *now* you can see why you really cannot sleep in my study."

"But…I don't understand. How—I thought we were pretty much in the middle of nowhere."

"Oh, we are. However, there's a very powerful satellite dish hidden amongst the castle ruins on the hill above our heads. Though, I do come here occasionally to restore my soul, there are a good many reasons why I can't afford to be out of touch with the world and the people I've left behind. Not completely, at any rate."

She stared at him as realization dawned, and the room seemed to shrink and grow darker around her. And then, with the impact of a wave thumping onto a hard sand beach, all the events of the past forty-eight hours came crashing in upon her, and her insides went sick and cold with dread. Through the ringing in her ears she heard her own voice.

"Have you…been in touch with…anyone? Since we got here?"

He nodded, his mouth grim. "I have."

"And…have you heard? Anything? About the boy, I mean. Your son. Is he—" She pressed her fingertips to her lips and swallowed past a painful sticky dryness in her throat, but couldn't bring herself to say the word.

Chapter 6

"He's alive," Corbett said. "For now." He turned abruptly to leave the room, plainly expecting her to follow.

"For *now?*" She hurried after him, her voice bumpy with conflicting emotions. "What does *that* mean?"

He closed the door to the study and took two strides into the now-empty kitchen before spinning to face her, moving like an out-of-balance wheel. "He survived the surgery. Apparently the bullet he took in the belly clipped some vertebrae on the way out. Did some damage to the spinal cord." His voice was quiet, but his eyes burned fierce and bright beneath a lock of hair that had fallen across his forehead. He raked it impatiently back with his fingers. "He's paralyzed. No way to tell if it's permanent until the swelling goes down."

"Oh, God." Lucia groped for support with one shaking hand and found the back of a chair. "Corbett, I'm so sorry. I never meant—"

"Oh, for the love of God, will you give off blaming yourself?" His words lashed out at her with a careless fury she'd never seen in him before, and she drew back, shocked. "The boy took a gun and went looking to kill someone with it and got himself shot, instead. Whose fault is that? His, I expect. And his mother's, for putting the hate in his heart. Mine for sure, for putting the hate in hers. It sure as hell wasn't yours. And somewhere in that frozen rock she calls a heart, the bi—the bloody woman knows it. It's not you she wants to hurt, anyway, though she won't hesitate to kill you if she thinks doing so will hurt me."

And would it hurt you, Corbett?

Stupid thing to ask. Of course it would. He cared deeply about all his agents, she knew that.

She whispered, "Why does she hate you so much?"

For a long suspenseful moment she waited, feeling the burn of those eyes and wondering. But then…the fire in them slowly died, and instead of answering her question he said gently, smiling a little, "I thought you wanted to have a look around."

She shook her head and gripped the chair back harder. "I deserve to know, Corbett. Since it appears your past has turned *my* life upside down."

He gave a soft huff of laughter that held no amusement. "Yes, I suppose you do."

But he realized as he said the words that even if it had not been so, he wanted very much to tell her… everything. He was a secretive man. By nature, he'd always thought. And this sudden desire to share with a

woman the most intensely personal events of his past—
and arguably those of which he was least proud—struck
him as very odd. Certainly out of character.

"I'll tell you what," he said, "since it's rather a long
story, why don't you go and put on your winter woolies,
and I'll bore you with it while we have a nice walk
outdoors. I don't know about you, but I could use a bit
of fresh air."

She gave him a long look before she turned and went
into her room, and he knew from the set of her chin she
wasn't about to let him off the hook. Of course, she had
no way of knowing he didn't *want* to be let off. He'd
kept his sins to himself for a long time. And he was
looking forward to this moment of confession.

Lucia wasted no time getting into the ski jacket and
boots Corbett had given her. Finding the cap in one of
the coat's pockets, she put that on, as well. When she
returned to the kitchen, she found Corbett ready and
waiting, bundled up in his sheepskin-lined coat and fur
hat, rifle in hand.

Neither of them said anything as he opened the door
and waited for her to go through ahead of him. As she
had very little recollection of her arrival the night before, she was interested to find herself in a windowless
but well-lit passageway. At the end of this another door
opened into what appeared to be a cellar, from which a
flight of wooden stairs led to a landing and yet another
door. Corbett, leading the way, gave a polite knock,
then opened the door into a kitchen very much like the
one they had just left.

"Kati and Josef live here," he said as he once again
held the door for her. "Though I doubt they'll be here

at the moment. Probably in their workshop—it's just across the yard." At Lucia's questioning look, he first closed the door to the cellar, then explained as he made his way through the quiet house ahead of her. "Josef used to work for the regional electric company, so he was able to do most of the electrical work on the cave house himself. Now that he's retired, he and Kati make handcrafted furniture and knickknacks for the summer tourist trade. He makes and Kati paints." He paused and waited for Lucia to catch up. "As you'll see when we get outside, this house sits on top of the only entrance to the cave. The only way, in or out, is through here."

"Except for the chimney," Lucia reminded him. He looked at her thoughtfully, and she said, *"What?"* beset by the kind of obscure guilt law-abiding people often feel in the presence of police officers. "I'm not exactly planning on trying it."

"I do hope you mean that. You'd mostly likely kill yourself, which would rather defeat my purpose in bringing you here, wouldn't it?" His expression was one she knew well: imperious…aloof.

She had a strong urge to slug him in the solar plexus, until she remembered he was already encumbered by fractured ribs. She said, instead, gesturing to the sofa in the room they were passing through, and the folded comforters piled on one end, "So this is where you slept last night, I presume?"

"Yes. Kati and Josef were kind enough to lend me their couch. And, *no,* you cannot sleep here instead," he added, as she was opening her mouth to suggest just that.

She was about to cast him a resentful look when her

eyes fell on the rifle he held cradled in his arms. "Of course not," she murmured demurely. "I know that."

"It's called protective custody. You, my dear, are the *protected*. I am the—"

"I said, I *know*," she snapped, glaring at him.

She has the heart of a lioness, Corbett thought, turning away to hide the admiration he felt for her. And the sympathy. *How she must hate this!*

He opened the cottage's front door and heard a small gasp from behind him. "Yes, I imagine it is a bit of a shock after being indoors where it's so warm, but once you get used to it, it's really quite—"

"Oh, wow."

He turned just as she moved out onto the porch steps, in time to see her face light up with wonder.

"It's so…*beautiful.*"

He glanced back at the view he'd seen so many times, in so many different seasons, and still never tired of: The snow-covered hillside with dark splotches of rocky outcroppings and small stands of evergreens, dropping away to the valley floor, shrouded now in a soft, wispy blanket of fog. The woods off to the right with outlines of trees like pen-and-ink sketches on downy-white paper, and to the left, the stone-cobbled lane looping down to the village, where red-tiled and reed-thatched roofs alike wore four-inch blankets of snow, and smoke rose in puffs from tall, stone chimneys.

He looked at Lucia again, saw her smile and the way her eyes sparkled and her nose, cheeks and chin bloomed red with the cold, and something tightened in his chest, his throat aching in unfamiliar ways.

"Beautiful," he said, "but a bit cold, I should imagine, for a girl raised in California."

She gave him an odd look—*almost resentful,* he thought—as she made her way down the steps, boots squeaking on the snow where Kati's and Josef's footsteps hadn't already crushed it.

"There's some fairly nice skiing hereabouts," he said in what he hoped was a winning way, because he felt an unaccustomed need to bring back the smile. "I know you don't ski, but I can teach you, if you'd like." Perhaps not as winning as he'd hoped. Rather stuffy, in fact. Like the teacher, as she'd forcibly reminded him recently, he no longer was.

It seemed she agreed, because the look she threw him was definitely not the one he'd hoped for.

"There are mountains in California," she said in an uneven voice as she trudged off down the snowy pathway to the front gate. "The fact that I don't ski isn't because I never had the opportunity to learn."

"Ah." He lengthened his stride in order to go ahead of her and unlatch the gate. "So why didn't you, if I might ask?"

On her way through the gate she paused almost in the wide half circle of his arms, and there was no mistaking the anger in the ice-blue eyes she raised to his. "You know *almost* everything there is to know about me, so I'm sure it didn't escape you that sports isn't exactly my *thing.* Remember? I'm the computer geek you hired right off the Berkeley campus. I don't ski, I don't ice skate, I don't row, I don't play tennis, I don't play racketball. I don't…do…sports."

"Yet you mastered several martial arts disciplines,"

he said evenly, "including some that are considered so lethal they're outlawed except for the military and law enforcement applications. So if you don't 'do sports,' it's not for lack of ability." She'd gone stalking off down the lane, arms waving like outriggers for balance, and he had to almost run to catch up with her.

"Look, you're obviously annoyed. Might I at least know what I've said or done to tick you off?"

She halted, tucking her bare hands under her arms and hugging herself for warmth, although he could see that shivers still wracked her. "You want to know what's bugging me? All right, I hate the fact that you know almost everything about me, and I don't know *squat* about you. Okay?"

"Oh, come on. You know—"

"I know your parents were born in Hungary, that they spied for Great Britain during the Cold War and fled in 1956, and that you and your brother were both born in London. I even know a bit about your dust-up with British Intelligence. I researched you before I took your job offer, of course—what did you expect? And it wasn't that easy, either, since Google hadn't been invented yet. But the truth is, I don't know who you are— as a person, I mean. All this—" her arms jerked out wide, then folded back around her again "—comes as a complete surprise to me. And the fact that you have a son—"

"Yes, well, as you know, that one came as a complete surprise to me, too," Corbett said dryly.

Her eyes widened in mock astonishment. "There, you see? I didn't even know you had a sense of humor. Or at least not with me."

"Oh, now wait—"

"And it's not…dammit, it's not just curiosity, either. Knowledge is power, right? Well, then, you have it all, don't you? And I have none. Do you know how that makes me feel? It makes me feel…*less.*"

"Good God. Less than *what?*"

"Less than you. Less than a grown-up. Just…less. As in, inferior."

"Inferior!" The word genuinely shocked him, and he could feel his own temper beginning to rise. "Oh, come now, let's not get too melodramatic. You know perfectly well that you, of all people, could not possibly be considered inferior to anyone, least of all me. You know I've never—" He broke off, grinning suddenly, bemused to discover his anger had dissipated before it had even fully formed. Impulsively, he gripped her arm, pulled her hand from its hiding place, wrapped it snugly in his and placed them both in his coat pocket, instead.

"Anyway," he said, as they set off at a comfortable clip down the snowy lane, "I do mean to begin to rectify the situation, immediately." He paused, frowned and added, "That is, if I can think where to start."

He glanced down and found her gazing at him in a way that did strange things to his pulse rate—something he might have enjoyed more if it hadn't been for the strain it was putting on his already aching ribs. He also felt a need to take a deep breath, something he couldn't have managed even if he'd had the courage to try, thanks to the layers of bandage still wrapped around his torso. Thinking of *that* brought back a memory of her warm and shower-fresh closeness that made him feel slightly light-headed, and he found that he was gripping her hand tightly inside his coat pocket. And that she was squeezing back.

He drew his hand and hers from his pocket with great reluctance, and for the sake of his sanity, let hers go. "I'll tell you what," he said in a garbled voice, "why don't you get the ball rolling? Ask me a question. Ask me anything." *Except about Cassandra DuMont,* he silently prayed. He'd need to work his way up to that one.

She hesitated, her blue eyes bright as she studied him. Then she turned and began walking again, more slowly this time, her hands tucked deep in the pockets of her—*his*—ski jacket. "All right, then, what about all this? The cottage, the cave, the castle, Kati and Josef—how did you come to have this place?"

"Ah—good one. Covers some family history, as well as a few of my own eccentricities. Well done."

"Stop stalling," she said darkly.

"I'm not, I swear." He placed a gloved hand flat over his heart. "It's just that I'm not used to this sort of thing. You can't expect me to simply open up the spigot and have all my secrets come pouring out."

"Oh, I can, and I do."

"Beastly woman," he muttered under his breath.

But there was a quirky tilt to the corner of his mouth and a glint in his eyes that made Lucia's heart lift and quiver with a lovely new excitement.

"All right, then. You say you already know my parents were spies for the Western Allies during the Cold War."

She nodded. He was holding one arm across his torso, and she slowed her step to a stroll to make it easier for him.

"They were living in Budapest at the time, newly

married, both of them working for the government—good registered members of the Communist Party—but they knew people in the business of spying couldn't count on any sort of future, and so when the opportunity came during the November uprising in 1956, they decided the time had come to leave. Kati's family had worked for my father's family for years. After the Russians 'liberated' Hungary in 1945, they fled north into these mountains and became craftsmen, as well as experts at lying low and staying off the government radar.

"I don't suppose I need to tell you how my parents fared in their new home. They were considered heroes of a sort in Great Britain, enjoying a certain degree of celebrity, which my father parlayed into a job with the foreign ministry, and eventually a seat in the House of Commons. My mother—well, you've seen how she's adapted. Anyway, they did keep their Magyar surname, but when my brother and I made our appearance they were bent on giving us good English names. Edward didn't fare badly—at least he shares his name with a whole lot of kings, and there is a Hungarian version. In my case, I can only wonder what they were thinking."

"What's wrong with Corbett? I like it—it means *raven,* doesn't it? So it suits you."

"Yes, and I suppose I did have this great wild shock of black hair when I was born. But there's simply no name equivalent in Hungarian—"

"What about the translation of raven?"

"*Holló?*" His grin was wry. "I don't know that it's much of an improvement. I've never heard of anyone named that, anyway. You may have noticed Kati and Josef call me *Lacsi,* which is the familiar form of Lazlo."

"Lot-zee," Lucia said, trying it out and nodding her approval. "Okay, getting back to how you came to own a hideout in a cave and a castle ruin…"

"Yes, yes, I'm getting to that, believe it or not, in my fashion."

And she could only catch her breath and hold it, wishing never to end this walk, loving the sound of his voice, the lightness of it…the easy way he smiled.

He cleared his throat portentously. "Meanwhile, back in the old country, communism fell and capitalism—which had never really gone away, you understand, merely underground—burst into full bloom. Tourism had been a thriving enterprise since the 1970s, when the Hungarian government declared amnesty for all those who'd fled in 1956. But now all those expatriots' children were returning to seek their roots, bringing along *their* children. A good many of them have bought property here, or inherited it.

"I found out about this particular piece through Kati and Josef. That village you see down there, looking so quaint and old-timey, is a very popular tourist spot in the summertime. The locals dress in traditional costume and entertain the tourists by plying the traditional trades and putting on folkdance festivals and whatnot. You have a similar place in the States, in Virginia, I believe—"

"Colonial Williamsburg," Lucia supplied.

"Yes, I believe that's right. Anyway, the rest of the time the people who live here are as much a part of the global village as anyone. And as much in danger of losing their way of life to runaway development. So when the villagers found out some firm was looking to build a big modern hotel and spa right above their little piece of paradise, they were understandably upset. That's when Kati and Josef contacted me about buying the place. Having just avoided prison by the skin of my teeth, a place to escape to seemed like rather a good idea to me." He shrugged. "And here we are."

"Yes," Lucia said absently. For her, his mention of the prison sentence he'd narrowly escaped had taken all the joy out of the day, as if a cloud had come up from nowhere to blot out the sun. "The charges of treason—you said you think this woman, Cassandra, is the one who framed you?"

"I don't think—I *know*," Corbett said grimly. "Though, I'm sure she had help. Particularly, since recent developments have uncovered all sorts of moles and leaks in the SIS."

She shivered suddenly, and, of course, he misunderstood.

"You're cold. We should head back."

"I'm fine." She pulled away from the hand he placed on her elbow. "You promised you'd tell me about Cassandra, and the minute her name comes up—"

"I did and I will," he said, and there was a certain tightness now around his mouth and a narrowing of his eyes. "But it's a long story, and it's colder than I expected. I'd rather neither of us froze to death while I'm telling it. Come on, let's go back. I could use something hot to drink about now, myself."

"What I'd love is a nice fire to warm my feet in front of," Lucia muttered, grudgingly accepting the helping hand he offered. She gave him a look along her shoulder. "Was there some reason why you didn't include one—and maybe a sitting room—in your hideaway?"

"I have a place to eat, a place to sleep, a place to work," he said with a shrug. "What else does anyone need?"

"What about a place to play? To relax? You know, put your feet up, read a book, have a glass of wine, listen to music, talk with a friend…" *Make out with someone you love…*

He frowned as he watched his boots crush the snow underfoot. "I have a comfortable chair in my study—sometimes I even put my feet up. If I want to listen to music, I can tune in to just about any satellite station. Sometimes I read there, or in bed. If I want a glass of wine or a chat with a friend, I generally do it in the kitchen. And as for play—" a smile came and went briefly "—I guess that's what I come outdoors for."

Clueless, Lucia thought, shaking her head. If she'd had any wild thoughts about seducing Corbett Lazlo in his cosy hideaway, her chances were looking rather bleak.

"I was never in love with her," Corbett said. "I say that not with pride, but with sadness. If I could have loved her, I believe some people—good people—would still be alive."

They were sitting at the kitchen table, kitty-corner from one another, hands curled around identical mugs of steaming hot coffee, carefully avoiding each other's eyes. When Corbett paused and raised his, Lucia lowered her lashes and lifted her mug to her lips. She would make no comment, ask no question that might interrupt the story he had to tell.

"I tell myself we were young—and we were, both of us. And typically heedless. Rash. We lied to each other, each for different reasons, and believed it wouldn't matter. But the fact is, it all began with that affair, and as a result of that affair, many people have been hurt. Not the least of whom is that poor boy. My son." He drank from his mug as though to wash a bitter taste from his mouth.

After a moment he went on, staring straight ahead at nothing. Or at his memories.

"As I guess you've already heard, Cassandra was sent by her father, Maximilian DuMont, to set me up for a hit. She engineered a chance meeting between us, which I gladly went along with. She was a real knockout, and I was, well, as *willing* as any young man." He shifted irritably in his chair. "I'm not going to go into the intimate details, if you don't mind. Suffice to say, it got very hot very quickly. As I said, we were both young and rash. I'm not sure, really, why she didn't arrange the hit right away. It would have been easy to do, since we didn't ID her as Max's daughter until after. Although I did have my suspicions. I wasn't *quite* so egotistical as to think it a natural everyday occurrence to have drop-dead gorgeous redheads falling over themselves to share my bed."

Lucia made a strangled sound and quickly drank more coffee.

Corbett glanced at her, then frowned and lifted his own mug before going on.

"Based on what I later learned, I think she'd convinced Max to let her string me along for a while, to see if she could get any valuable information about SIS operations out of me before bumping me off. It didn't work out that way, as you already know."

Lucia cleared her throat. "She fell in love with you."

He nodded. "She did. I knew it but didn't think a thing about it. What did I know about a woman's love? What the hell, I was enjoying myself—and her. She was unlike any woman I'd ever known—exciting…a bit dangerous, you know?

"Anyway, we'd been at it about six weeks when Daddy decided he'd waited long enough and ordered her to lead me into the ambush he'd set up. Instead, she warned me." He paused to scrub a hand over his eyes. "My God, when I think what it must have cost her to do that—to go against her own father, knowing what he was capable of… But at the time I didn't care. I was following my own agenda. And I saw a chance to set a trap of my own to take down DuMont's organization. I used her."

He lifted his head to glare at Lucia, and his eyes looked as though they'd been burned into their sockets. "We had this big emotional scene. I pretended to be devastated that she'd lied to me. Outraged. Angry. Then I forgave her. We made up, and I gave her a ring. Supposedly my fraternity ring. Except it had been especially made for the occasion by the magicians at SIS, a very nice little bug. Quite clever, really. She couldn't wear it openly, of course, so I gave it to her on a chain, which she could wear concealed under her clothes— close to her heart, as it were. Then I sent her back to her father." He drank some coffee, then grimaced.

"I truly don't know what I expected to happen. I suppose I knew there was a possibility he'd kill her, even if she *was* his daughter. As it turned out, he did worse."

"Adam said he disowned her," Lucia said, and her voice was only a scratchy whisper.

"Oh, yes. He did that. But before he gave her the

boot, he put together a hit squad to take me out. Her brother was the one in charge of the team, and Cass was forced to go along so she could watch me die. But because of the bug, we were ready and waiting for them. So instead of watching me die, Cassandra DuMont watched me kill her brother."

He pushed away his empty coffee cup and, after a moment, covered his face with both hands. His voice came muffled and hollow. "I'll never forget the look on her face when she realized what I'd done. She knew I had to have gotten the information about the hit through her, somehow. She was a smart girl, and she put it together in a heartbeat. She knew I'd used her…betrayed her. I'm certain now that she also knew at the time she was pregnant with my child. She was only nineteen, Lu. *Nineteen.* She was just a girl, crazy in love with me. And I destroyed her."

Chapter 7

Oh, God, no wonder he's the way he is. No wonder he can't let himself love me. Love anyone.

"Oh, God…"

It wasn't until she realized Corbett was staring at her with eyes hot and red-rimmed and a jaw tight with self-loathing that she knew she had spoken aloud. And that he'd misunderstood.

Stricken, she put out her hand to touch his arm, opened her mouth to explain. But he'd already pushed back from the table, away from her. Rising, he began to pace, one hand folded across his ribs, the other, with fingers spread, raking roughly through already unkempt hair.

"I know what you think of me, and I don't blame you—believe me, I've thought the same thing myself at least a thousand times. It was a reprehensible, truly beastly thing to do. And yet I—" he turned to look at her, his face bleak "—I've thought what I might have done differently, if I were in the same spot today. And God help me, I can't see what I would change. Even if I had loved her, I had a job to do. A duty…"

He paused, swore, then went silent, listening. He strode to the door of his study and opened it, and then, above the hum of tension inside her head, Lucia could hear it, too. A high-pitched electronic beeping. Still muttering under his breath, Corbett vanished into his study, leaving Lucia to sag in her chair and rest her forehead on her cupped hand, drained.

He called me Lu.

It the midst of the emotional blitz, it had slipped by her. How could she not have noticed? In the ten years she'd worked for Corbett Lazlo, often close by his side, he'd never once called her anything but Lucia—and an occasional *Miss Cordez* when he was particularly impatient with her. Today he'd called her *Lu.* The implications of that, together with the confession…

Things are different between us. Just like that. From one day to the next, everything's changed.

She felt hollow and shivery inside, the same way she'd felt in Corbett's shower, in Paris. It was a feeling as much of fear as of happiness. *Too much, too fast. It scares me.*

"Lucia, sorry—can you come here for a minute, please? I'm going to need you."

Corbett called to her from the doorway of his study, but turned away before she could respond. He didn't want to see her expression when she looked at him. Disgust or disappointment—he didn't know which would be worse, but he was certain either would cause him pain more searing than his broken ribs, and he didn't know whether he was strong enough just now to maintain his composure in the face of it.

He eased himself gingerly into a chair in front of the bank of monitors, acutely aware that she'd come into the room, that she was there close by his side—too close.

"What is it? Is it the boy?" Her voice sounded breathless and shaken.

He aimed a brief glance at the tawny curl just in front of her left ear and shook his head. "I don't know yet. It's Adam—"

"Adam! Oh, no…please, no!"

Her stricken cry stabbed him like a knife. Not that it surprised him. He'd wondered and then there was that rather intimate little moment between them when they'd said goodbye before she'd boarded the helicopter….

"Nothing like that," he said quickly, aware that his smile must appear strained, even grim. *And how will I be able to tolerate being around them if—when—they both figure out they're in love with each other?* "As far as I know, at this moment Adam is fine. He wants a video conference. Can you route it for us so it can't be traced?"

There was a small pause, a throat-clearing sound and then a calm, "Yes, of course."

She pulled a chair over from his desk, sat in it and reached for the keyboard.

He watched, transfixed, as she began to tap at the keys, her fingers flying too fast to follow, a little frown creasing her forehead, color still staining her cheeks.

The smell of her hair clouded his mind. When he couldn't stand it anymore, he rose, stiffly.

"Call me," he said as he headed for the door. "When you have it set up."

"This might take a while." She tossed a glance over her shoulder. "Where will you be?"

He paused, considering how much to tell her about the one place he knew he would find the solitude he needed just now, and finally settled on a rather prim, "I believe I'll have a wash."

"Oh." She chewed her lower lip for a moment, looking uncertain. "Do you want to use the shower? The one in my—in *your*—bathroom?"

"No," he said. "Thank you." And he went out, shutting the door firmly behind him.

Lucia sat for a few minutes, biting her lip and staring at the closed door, before she turned back to the computer screen. For a while she was able to lose herself in the task of routing a video connection through a spider's web of encryptions and dummy hosts and red herrings. At last, satisfied the system was hack-proof, she contacted Adam and left him a message, then went, with nervous flutters in her stomach, to find Corbett.

The kitchen was empty and silent, the kind of silence that seems almost to have weight and substance. Lucia had lived by herself for ten years and liked it, but she'd never felt so wretchedly *alone*. And acutely aware, for the first time, that she was, in fact, in a cave.

She debated what to do—whether to go to Josef and Kati's house and try to find Corbett. He must be finished with his "wash" by this time, she reasoned. Then she thought she might use the solitude to take a much-needed shower herself. She went into her bedroom and was in the process of collecting her toiletries and a selection of clean clothes when the flashlight rolled out of the suitcase and onto her foot. Swearing, she bent to rub her bruised instep, then picked up the flashlight. And as she felt the familiar shape of it in her hand, a new idea came to her.

This is a cave. I'm in a cave, and there's only one way out.

Except for the chimney.

What if…

Yes, what if?

She stared down at the flashlight, biting her lip. She was alone. Corbett was taking a bath. She might not have a chance like this again to explore the back of the cave. A chance to find the chimney. Just in case, she told herself. *In case I need another way out. I should know where it is.*

Resolved that what she was doing was the right thing, Lucia made her way confidently back through the kitchen and storeroom. It wasn't until she had shut the storeroom door behind her and turned on her flashlight that her heart began to beat faster. The light seemed small in the immense darkness…and yet, as her eyes grew more accustomed to it, she realized the darkness wasn't as complete as she'd thought it would be. In fact, there seemed to be some sort of light source farther into the cave. An emergency light, maybe? Or, like the air currents, could it be coming from the chimney?

A sense of adventure filled her, wiping out any remaining traces of doubt. She began to make her way deeper into the cave, moving carefully, watching her feet on the rocky, uneven floor. Odd, she thought, the way one's perceptions changed when one was alone in the darkness. The sulfur smell she'd noticed earlier seemed much stronger now, and the tiniest sounds seemed enormous. And the light…yes, it was definitely getting brighter. It almost had to be a lantern of some kind, but that didn't seem likely. Did it?

She stopped, strained her ears to listen. But all she heard was the faint sound of water flowing over rock. The thermal spring Corbett had told her about, surely. It sounded quite close now, and…yes, she could see wisps of steam rising in the golden glow that outlined the rock formations directly ahead. These formations were quite remarkable, and ordinarily she'd have been fascinated with them, but at the moment she was completely focused on discovering the mysterious source of light. If the household did get its hot water from these springs, she supposed it would make sense to have a source of illumination available, in case someone needed to work on the plumbing. Or in case… For a moment her heart seemed to stop. *In case someone wanted to use the springs to take a bath?*

The notion, and its immediate implications, arrived too late. Moving quickly and silently, she'd already rounded the last of the stalactites, stalagmites—she could never remember which was which—between her and the thermal spring. She could now see that it flowed into a natural rock basin, its sides stained lovely shades of blue and green and white by the minerals in the crystal clear water. And there, stretched out full-length, relaxing in the shallow pool, his body burnished gold by the light of the lantern he'd placed on a rock ledge nearby, was Corbett.

A hiss of shock burst from her lips as she stepped reflexively backward, and her foot found an uneven place in the cave floor. She grabbed for a stalactite—or was it a stalagmite?—and the flashlight slipped from her hand and rolled away into crazily leaping shadows.

Corbett jerked around and nearly passed out from the pain caused by the jolting movement of his unprotected ribs. Through the dark blotches interfering with his vision, he could make out Lucia's face, pale and oddly shadowed, and the indecision clearly written there. Had he not been breathless with agony, he might have found it amusing to watch the battle being played out between the natural impulse of a compassionate woman to rush to the aid of someone in pain, and the equally natural human impulse to turn away from the unexpected sight of someone naked—particularly a member of the opposite sex.

"Oh, G-G-God, Corbett," she stammered, "I'm s-so sorry. Truly, I am. I didn't know…" There was a pause, and then a fearful, "Are you all right?"

He was afraid to take another breath and hadn't enough left of the last one for words, so he just shook his head. He was beyond caring about modesty, or the fact that she probably hated the sight of him anyway, right about now. He closed his eyes, gritted his teeth and concentrated all his effort on producing sound.

"I'm sorry to ask it of you, but I'm afraid I'm going to need a bit of help," he managed to say, with slow and stiff formality. "If you wouldn't mind handing me that towel, over there."

He heard only silence. He turned, or tried to, and managed to shift himself around enough so that he

could see her without twisting his torso too much. He
watched her pick up the towel, moving slowly, like
someone underwater. Or was that only his pain-warped
vision? Then she turned, and he realized with a shock
that she was angry. *Furious.*

"Look," he croaked, "I do apologize. It's just that I
don't think I'm going to be able to get out of here without help."

Again, there was only silence. Then, holding the
towel in both hands like a peculiar weapon of some
kind, she began to walk toward him. A little thrill ran
through him as he watched her eyes. She looked like a
lioness, he thought, moving in for the kill.

She came as far as the edge of the pool. He braced
himself, heart thumping painfully against his ribs, having no earthly idea what she was going to do next. She
paused for a long suspenseful moment, gazing down at
him. Then she pressed her lips together and dropped the
towel in a heedless heap beside him, obviously not
caring that she'd gotten part of it wet in the process.

"Do you know what you are?" Her voice was low and
raspy, rather resembling a lion's purr, in fact. "You are
the world's biggest *idiot*—and considering the state of
the world that's saying a *lot*. The only thing I can't understand is why I didn't figure out sooner what a bloody
idiot you are. I was a grown-up woman the day you met
me, Corbett Lazlo, and I've been in love with you for
just about that long." She grabbed at a breath. "You've
known that, and you've insisted on treating me like a
schoolgirl with a silly crush. And you know what *really*
gets me? You definitely feel *something* for me—that's
pretty obvious. You almost kissed me yesterday, don't

deny it. Maybe it's just chemistry, or whatever. I just figured it out. I think you love me, too. Yes, you do. But you've got this crazy idiotic idea that—I don't know, maybe *you* aren't allowed to be happy, or you think… I don't know what you think. But you know what? You can get your own damn self out of that damn *tub.*"

Then, while he stared at her, incredulous, she turned and left him there.

Lucia sat at the keyboard, still shaking. Still not able to believe she'd done what she'd done. Said what she'd said.

How could I have been so stupid?

What if I was wrong?

She had been so certain, there in the dim light of the cave, staring down at his long, lean body in the pristine water. Remembering all the moments…the signs…the clues she'd dismissed as wishful thinking. Even before that crazy heart-stopping moment in his closet, there'd been so many times, so many things she should have paid more attention to. The way his heart felt, thumping against her chest when he'd bested her in a martial arts match. The way he'd glared and then grown frosty on those rare occasions she'd told him she had a date. And *this*—whisking her away to his own private hideaway to protect her when anyone else would have been sent to a safe house somewhere.

Now, in the familiar cold light of a computer monitor, staring at the patiently blinking cursor, she wished with all her heart that she could go back and undo what had just happened.

If only, she thought, life had an escape key.

If I'm wrong about him, then in his mind I've just proven he was right all along—I am nothing but a silly schoolgirl with a crush.

How overwrought she must have sounded, especially to someone with his incredible self-control.

How would she be able to face him now? What would she say to him when she saw him next?

It would depend, she supposed, on what *he* said to *her. That's it—that's what I'll do. I'll wait and pick up my cue from him.*

I wish he'd come, dammit. Let's get this over with.

What's taking him so long? What if he really can't *get out of that basin? What if—*

She was teetering on the edge of panic when she heard the door next to the study open…then close. Her whole body froze—except for her heart, and that part of her anatomy seemed to have gone a little berserk. Behind her the study door opened. She waited, and it quietly closed.

I won't look, she thought. And then, *No—that's too childish.*

She threw one brief, reckless look over her shoulder and said tartly, "I see you made it."

Facing the computer screen again, she closed her eyes. *Oh, God, he looks so pale. He really is hurting—physically and emotionally. I shouldn't have hit him with this. Not now.*

Without comment, he came and pulled out the chair next to hers and carefully lowered himself into it. When he was settled, he nodded toward the screen. "I take it you have the connection?" His voice was as it always was when addressing her: formal, controlled, calm. As if nothing out of the ordinary had happened between them.

Anger spurted anew into Lucia's blood and pounded its way through her veins.

"Of course," she said. *Show some emotion, damn you. I know you feel. Show* something.

She tapped viciously at the keyboard and a moment later Adam's face filled the monitor.

"G'day, gorgeous." The words didn't quite match the jerky movement of his image, but his grin was irrepressible as usual. "Oops—sorry, mate. Didn't see you were there, too."

"Yeah, right...*mate.*" Corbett's voice was dry, his breath a soft whisper along her cheek as she watched his image join hers in the small window at the bottom left of the screen. She closed her eyes and held her breath, then realized Adam would be able to see that, too. "You have a report for me." It wasn't a question. Corbett's mouth had settled into a grim line.

"Yeah...right." Adam's grin vanished, as well. "News from the hospital is, the boy's awake and alert. Still paralyzed, though. Mum's been at his bedside, but that hasn't kept her from directing all-out war against our guys. It's amazing what you can discover when you know what you're looking for. Seems our girl Cassandra has taken over the reins of S.N.A.K.E. And there is some word on the street that *taken* from dear old Dad is the operative word. For now, everyone's in hiding, including me." There was a pause, while Adam fidgeted. "And we had a bit of a security breach this morning."

Corbett's body tensed. "Where? How bad?"

"Here—headquarters. Not too bad. We stopped 'em before they got very far."

Lucia's gasp was overridden by Corbett's oath. "A *break-in?* Impossible."

"Nope, 'fraid not, mate."

"How'd they get in? Not through the garage. Our security—"

Adam's head moved jerkily from side to side. "Nope, the roof. Your apartment, actually. Broke in through the skylight. Didn't get any farther than the elevator, though."

Corbett snapped a look at Lucia, who glared back at him. His voice was a furious growl. "Who knew about that skylight? Damnation. This has to be coming from someone—"

"Not necessarily," Adam interrupted. "Once they'd pinpointed the building, the skylight would be the logical way in, wouldn't it?"

Corbett swore again. "Tell me you took care of the intruders?"

Adam's grin reappeared, and this time it wasn't pleasant. "Goes without sayin', boss. Unfortunately, none survived our people's particular brand of TLC, so if we do have a mole, we won't find out who it is from them."

"Pity." There was a pause, during which Lucia watched Adam's image shift awkwardly. She felt Corbett take a deep breath and heard it catch when the pain hit him. "Any more casualties on our side?" Adam shook his head. Corbett snarled, "Don't lie to me, man."

There was another pause, and then Adam said in a cheerful voice that was only partly undermined by his crooked smile. "Under the circumstances I'll make allowances for that remark, mate. We both know I'm not above a gentle fib on occasion, but I've never lied to you, now, have I?" The smile vanished altogether. "Truth is, I don't know, okay? Tom Schroeder called in en route to a safe house, but he never got there. At this point, that's all I know." His grin flashed for a jerky second. "How are *you* doing? Those ribs feeling any better?"

In the small window on the monitor screen, Lucia saw Corbett's eyes dart toward her, then as quickly away. She opened her mouth, but before she could say a word, he bit out a savage, "I'm *fine*. My ribs are *fine*. If you don't mind, can we not waste time talking about my bloody *ribs?*"

"Sure, boss. Right-O, boss. Any instructions, boss?"

"Find me that mole!" Corbett snarled, and pushed his chair back out of the camera's range.

"What the hell's eating—"

Lucia cut him off with a hurried, "Signing off, Adam. Watch your back." She clicked the mouse and his image vanished. Another click closed down the connection. She swiveled her chair to face Corbett, who had gotten to his feet and was pacing restlessly with one hand in his pocket, the other folded protectively across his ribs.

"Would you mind telling me what *that* was all about?"

In a windowless room deep in the bowels of the Lazlo Group headquarters, Adam sat staring at the entwined pentagrams that made up the organization's logo outlined on a huge blue monitor, while muttering to himself.

"What the bloody hell was *that* all about?"

He'd never known Laz to be so edgy before. But then, he'd never known him to be cooped up with a woman day and night, before, either—particularly one he was too stubborn to admit he was crazy in love with.

Adam had felt the tension between them even through the computer screen. Something had happened between those two. Or was about to. He knew, as surely as he would have known if a thunderstorm was about to hit.

Bleakly, he tapped a key and the computer whined into silence.

"Why are you treating Adam like this is all his fault?" Lucia persisted, after Corbett had favored her with one of his superior looks. "He's not to blame for what's been happening."

He looked for a moment as if he would fire off another scathing denial. But then she saw the light in his eyes slowly die, and the lines of his face grow long and strained as he paused to grip the back of a chair and lean his weight on it. "I sincerely hope you're right," he said softly.

A wave of cold shuddered through her stomach. "Oh, you can't seriously think—you can't possibly think *Adam's* the mole."

His desolate eyes flicked across her face and then moved on, settling on nothing. "It has to be someone close to me. Someone *very* close. There aren't that many people who know about that skylight."

"But what he said is true. Once they'd accessed the roof—"

"Yes," he said, straightening and rubbing his eyes tiredly, "and he was quick to point that out, wasn't he?

But why would anyone think the rooftop would be the best way in? How would they know to try that first?"

She couldn't bear the acute misery written in every line and shadow on his face. "It's not Adam," she said firmly, her own anger with him draining away like water in sand. "I know it's not. It must be someone else. It has to be."

"Who, then?"

"I don't know, who else knows about the skylight?"

"Besides Adam? Me, my brother Edward, the people who installed it, I suppose, although there's no reason they'd know who it belonged to, since the work order was channeled through the bank on the ground floor. And," he added after a moment, "now you."

She drew a sharp reflexive breath, as if a gust of wind had struck her in the face. "You don't—"

"No," he said softly, an odd little smile touching his lips, "I don't."

"What about Edward?"

"No." He said it with flat certainty. "Not that I don't think Edward's scruples can be bought. For one thing, he, uh… Well the truth is, his bad habits do tend to keep him chronically short of cash. But he's my brother. He'd never do anything to hurt me. Never."

"Girlfriends, then?" She said it stiffly, pushing it past the pain that had come to wrap itself around her heart.

He looked at her for a moment, and his lips curved in a sardonic smile. "Believe it or not, no. You're the only woman I've ever invited into that bedroom."

She opened her mouth but words refused to come. She stared at him while the moment stretched into unknown minutes, counted in the thumping beats of her heart. His eyes seemed to catch fire and shimmer back into hers.

It was the kind of moment that can't possibly drift away into nothing. A moment like that must have a re-sounding conclusion, must end with a bang, an action or words that change everything. Either that, or…an interruption.

Like a tap on the door, and the door opening, and Kati's face, wreathed with smiles, and her voice singing out in cheerily defiant Hungarian, *"Kész az ebéd!"*

Which even Lucia knew meant it was time for lunch.

"I just refuse to believe Adam would ever betray you," Lucia said. "It has to be someone else, and I'd like a chance to try and find out who, that's all."

It was the next morning, the first time Corbett had been alone with her since her emotional—and, he was sure, deeply regretted—outburst the day before. As it turned out, the "lunch" Kati had interrupted them to an-nounce would be the main meal of the day, since it was already midafternoon. And she'd outdone herself, as usual, with a spread that included everything from stuffed cabbage rolls and chicken paprika to the rolled crepes called *palacsinta* she always made when he came because she knew he was fond of them. Anyway, she always had a tendency to go all-out when Corbett was in residence, and having another woman to show off for had no doubt only prodded her to even greater efforts.

Josef had joined them, as well, so conversation was sprightly and filled with all the world news and local gossip. And since it was mostly in Hungarian—Josef's English being much less fluent than his wife's—Lucia had contented herself with smiling and nodding, watching and listening. And, Corbett was sure, soaking up a great deal more than anyone suspected, given that remarkable mind of hers, until she'd begun to nod off over coffee and Kati's homemade pastries. Even geniuses, it seemed, needed their rest now and then.

As Corbett studied "his" genius now, he recognized the stubborn set of her mouth and, realizing she'd do it whether she had his okay or not, nodded. "Fine. Go ahead."

But as she started to swivel back to the computer, he placed both hands on the arms of her chair to stop her. "However, not right now. I have something to show you. Come—get dressed."

"I am dressed."

Pouting, her lips were so tempting he could feel juices begin to pool at the back of his throat. "Hmm," he said, swallowing a remark he knew he'd regret, "I can see that. I meant put on your coat and mittens. It's outside."

She cocked a wary eye toward him. "Oh, God. What is it? Not skis. I said—"

"It's not skis, I promise. But you're going to have to come outside to see it."

"I'd rather not. I can do much more good right here. If I—"

"I have no doubt of that. However, you could also do with some fresh air. Come—up you get."

Her chin rose another notch, and he realized there were now only scant inches separating his mouth from hers. He grew light-headed at the thought.

"You're not—"

"—Your teacher," he said, straightening up before he

did something he'd regret even more than words. "I know. You've already reminded me of that fact. However, you are in my protective custody, which makes me your custodian. I am also, as you seem to forget, your boss. I will expect you bundled up and on the front steps in—" he drew back his cuff to glance at his watchless-wrist "—five minutes. Do I make myself clear?"

"Perfectly."

"Good." He turned away to hide his smile, feeling ridiculously buoyant, considering he could feel her furious glare burning holes between his shoulder blades.

Chapter 8

It was more like fifteen minutes later when Lucia ventured onto the clean-swept front steps of Josef and Kati's cottage, grumbling under her breath, hugging herself and shivering theatrically. Corbett, who had obviously been pacing, judging from the path his footsteps had worn in the snow, gave her an annoyed stare, which warmed her heart considerably.

The truth was, she felt invigorated, and not the least bit cold. She knew she was playing a risky game, taunting him so, particularly since she didn't know him well enough to be able to predict what his reaction might be under these unaccustomed circumstances. Since her impassioned declaration of love, which obviously hadn't fazed him, she'd felt a new sense of freedom. As if a reckless and wicked imp had come to sit on her shoulder and was constantly whispering in her ear, What have you got to lose?

It was another lovely sunny morning, cold and sparkling, looking more than ever like a pen-and-ink drawing with snow still lying thick on the ground but melted off rooftops and the black skeletons of trees. Refusing to acknowledge the beauty of it, Lucia focused instead on the object on the ground near Corbett's feet.

"What," she inquired darkly, "is that?"

He reared back, as if astounded by her ignorance. "It's a sled."

"Uh-huh. Where did you find it?"

"It was in the outbuilding." Bending down, he picked up the gleaming wood-and-metal contraption by one end and bumped it against the ground to dislodge the bits of muddy snow that were clinging to its runners. "We dug it out last night, Josef and I, after you passed out at the dinner table."

He'd spent hours cleaning and oiling it, actually. In a way, it had been therapy for him, working methodically with his hands and thinking about everything that had happened that day.

Everything. Thinking about her, mostly. And Adam. The possibility one of them could have betrayed me. Telling myself it couldn't be her. Not Lucia.

Asking himself when she could possibly have done it. Then remembering that she'd been alone in the cave house all night that first night. Knowing that with her computer knowledge she could easily have sent off a message…

No. I won't believe it. I know I don't know her as well as I thought I did, but still… My God, look at her.

Even bundled up and red-nosed, her body round and as shapeless as a bear's, she was still so adorable she made his throat ache with a repressed urge to laugh out loud. Even when she directed a frigid stare at the sled, then at him, and said frostily, "What part of 'I don't do sports' don't you understand?"

Lifting his gloved hands to his mouth to cover a smile, Corbett huffed out a cloud of freezing vapor, then said in a stern but patient teacher's voice he knew would annoy her, "This is not sports. It's a child's toy. All you have to do is sit on the thing. Or you can even lie down on it. Look." He dropped the sled onto the snow, gingerly lowered his backside onto it, grasped the rope holds on the sides and leaned back. "You see? You steer with your feet—like this."

She folded her arms on her chest and shook her head. "Oh, no—no way. I watch the Olympics. I've seen the people that do this sort of thing. I thought they were crazy. And they were wearing helmets. No way, Jose."

"All right, suit yourself." He got up, dusted off his pants and bent down to pick up the sled's pull rope. As he started walking toward the gate, he heard ski boots clomp down the wooden steps behind him.

"All right, since you've got me out here… Hey, wait, hold up a minute, okay?"

Wearing what he hoped was a look of long-suffering and not a reflection of the satisfaction he felt, he paused and waited for her to catch up. "I want to see the castle," she said, breathing hard, cold-reddened lips making charming vapor puffs in the frosty air. "You did say you'd show it to me."

"Ah. So I did." He made a great show of thinking it over. "All right, here's the deal. I'll take you up and show you the castle, if you agree to come down—" he tugged on the sled's rope, lifting it a few inches off the snow "—on this."

She cocked her head, bit down on her lower lip and looked at him for a moment, then answered, "Deal," so readily he knew she was already thinking of ways to get out of it.

The hike up the mountain to the castle ruins was less strenuous than Lucia had expected. For one thing, for someone accustomed to California's Sierra Nevada, it wasn't much of a mountain—more of a hill, really. And then the path, which was wide enough in most places to be called a road, wound upward in a gentle spiral that afforded them everwidening views of the snowy hills and woods that surrounded them, and the valley and villages far below. As they trudged unhurried along the path, making new footprints in the undisturbed snow, Corbett had plenty of time to fill her in on the area's history and geography, some of which she already knew from her own research. By mutual, though unspoken, agreement, they didn't mention their own complex pasts, or the consequences affecting their immediate future. The Lazlo Group, Cassandra DuMont, her son Troy, Adam Sinclair and Paris—those things seemed far away, though not at all out of mind, like a bank of thunderclouds piled up on distant mountains.

The castle, Corbett told her, most likely dated from the Turkish Wars, sometime in the fifteenth or sixteenth century. It was thought to have been a relatively minor military outpost and not worth the effort to excavate or restore.

"If it had been," Corbett said, "I doubt the Hungarian powers that be would have been willing to let it pass into private hands. So, naturally, I'm quite satisfied with it as it is."

They had emerged from the last small stand of forest onto the edge of the rocky, windswept summit.

"There's not much to see," Lucia said, trying to hide her disappointment.

He snorted as he plodded past her, towing the sled. "Not if you were expecting Disneyland. All these rocks you see—" he waved one arm in a wide sweep "—were once part of the walls and battlements. Most of the part that's still standing is over here, on the lee side of the hill—maybe because it's a bit more protected from the wind and weather. Over the centuries nature's taken a much greater toll than the Turks ever did. Here, I'll show you."

He half turned and held out his hand, and she gasped and caught at a breath as if a gust of wind had snatched it from her. Seeing him there, tall against a backdrop of scudding clouds, his eyes vivid mirrors of the patches of blue sky, jaws dark with stubble and cheeks reddened by the cold, wind riffling the fur on his hat and collar, she felt a wave of desire so intense and raw it rocked her like an unexpected blow. Stunned her, so that she reached blindly and let him take her hand and pull her, unprotesting, against his side.

"See there?" he said, pointing, and through the haze of her passion-fogged senses she could see the definite outline of a rough square in the snow. "That's the foundation of one of the towers. And over there is another one."

She drew an unsteady breath and gulped. "Oh, wow."

Having recovered most of her wits, she pulled away from him and went slipping and sliding down a short embankment to where a tumble of squareish blocks ended in an upright section of wall. As she came closer to the yard-thick wall she saw that it stood a good bit higher than her head, except for one squared-off section about chin height that could only have been a window. She was trying without success to hoist herself onto the ledge when Corbett came to join her.

"Determined to break your neck, are you?"

Still trembling inside, she smiled winningly at him over one shoulder. "Come on—give me a leg up. I'll bet the view is amazing from up here."

"Hmm, rather intrepid for someone who doesn't do sports." But she caught a thrilling glimpse of a grin before he laced his gloved fingers together and bent down to offer them as a foothold.

She placed the toe of her boot in the cradle of his hands and one hand on his shoulders, held her breath… and a moment later, gave a small squawk of surprise as she found herself perched in the opening of the ancient wall.

"Oh, man…" She rose unsteadily to her feet, bracing against a wave of vertigo with one hand on each side of the opening. "This really is cool. You should see…" She leaned to see more, but pulled back at a strangled sound from Corbett. "What?"

He was shaking his head and staring resolutely at the ground. "Nothing. Do go on."

"Well, you can see Kati and Josef's cottage from here, did you know that? It's directly below us. I guess that means—" she turned in the opening and pointed back toward the ruins "—the chimney must come out somewhere over there."

"It would, if it went up in a straight line, like a man-made chimney." He held up his arms and made a beckoning gesture. "However, since it was made by Mother Nature, and nature, as they say, abhors straight lines—"

"A vacuum."

"I beg your pardon?"

"Nature abhors a vacuum. I suppose she could also have a thing against straight lines, although I've—"

"Oh, do shut up," Corbett said cheerfully. "I'll be happy to show you where it comes out, if you insist. But first, please come down from there before you hurt yourself. There's a good—"

His last word was lost—fortunately for him, as far as Lucia was concerned—in a grunt of mixed surprise and pain as she dropped from the window ledge straight into his arms.

She murmured, gazing into his eyes with deep concern, "I forgot about your ribs. I hope I didn't hurt you."

"I'll survive," he said, without benefit of breath. Although, the longer he stood there holding her and looking down into her eyes, the less aware he was of either the pain in his ribs or the lack of air in the lungs beneath them. It took willpower he didn't know he had to drag himself back from the brink of insanity. "I have just one question, though. Why this obsessive interest in ancient geothermal rock formations?"

She drew back—as he'd hoped and prayed she would, since he lacked the moral strength to push her away—and stared at him with a look of puzzlement. "I'm interested, yes. You told me about it, and I found it fascinating. I want to see it. I'm curious—wouldn't you be?"

He stared at her a moment longer, then conceded stiffly, "All right, yes, I suppose I would be." He turned around and pointed. "See there, that curved wall, that's an old cistern." He started walking toward it and she fell in beside him, listening intently.

Too intently? Why?

He gave himself a mental shake and went on with his lecture.

"Built to collect rainwater, probably sometime later than the castle itself. I imagine the original inhabitants of the castle were in the process of digging themselves a cistern when they broke through to the cave underneath. They wouldn't have bothered to finish building the thing, since now they had a ready source of both water and escape. Later on, though, this cave, and the others in the region, were used by all sorts of people—smugglers, rebels, refugees—who might have had good reasons to want to hide the entrance to the tunnel. So—" he paused at the edge of the crumbling rock wall that surrounded what appeared to be a shallow, hand-dug well about ten feet deep "—they built the cistern around it. As I said, though, the tunnel, or chimney, or whatever you want to call it, hasn't been used in years. I don't know if it's even passable. And," he quickly added, as Lucia leaned to peer over the side, "I don't intend to start exploring it now, in case you were thinking of weaseling out of our deal and hoping to get home that way."

She looked up at him and said quickly, "I wasn't thinking any such thing. I'm not completely crazy." She backed away from the ruined wall, brushing snow from her gloved hands, and he noticed she'd began to shiver.

"You're cold," he said gently, smiling a little, both at her automatic glare of denial and his equally reflexive urge to pull her close and warm her. "Are you ready to go home?"

Lucia tucked her hands into the pockets of her borrowed ski jacket and glared at him with dark foreboding. While it was true that most of her objection to the sled had been a put-on, merely a way of taunting Corbett, there was a knotted-up feeling in her stomach that was all too real. And all too familiar. It was the same feeling she got whenever she thought of the way her relationship with him—the way her life—was changing. *Too fast!* Thrilling, yes, but not quite under her control. And getting on that sled with Corbett had begun to seem rather like an analogy for it all.

"Oh, all right," she said in a grumpy tone she hoped would hide the fact that her heart was pounding and her breathing had become quick and shallow. "But just so you know, if we run into a tree and kill ourselves, it's on your head."

"No trees," he said cheerfully, pointing toward the place he'd chosen for their descent. "See?"

"Oh, my God," said Lucia. Straight down was what it looked like to her. All the way to the first loop of the road. Then another straight drop to the lane that ran past Josef and Kati's cottage. She turned a horrified look on Corbett. "You must be kidding."

"Not at all. It's not as steep as it looks, you know. It's all a matter of perspective."

"Insane, then," she muttered. "Completely mad."

"Oh, come now. This from the woman who attacked an armed man with nothing but her bare hands and feet. Here—you don't need to do a thing except hold on. Sit right here." He guided her gently but firmly until she was perched on the sled, arms and legs pointing in all directions, like a newborn calf's. "Okay, relax. Now, put your feet here, in the middle of the bar. I'll do the steering."

She caught and held a breath as the sled began to move, then stopped, teetering now on the very edge of what seemed to her like a precipice. A cliff. She caught another breath when she felt him settle himself behind her and align his legs alongside hers, fold one arm around her and bring her close against his chest. With the other he took a firm hold on the tow rope. She felt his body rock back…then sharply forward.

"O-o-oh…my…Go-o-d…"

The earth dropped out from under her and all the breath in her body emerged in one long wail of sheer terror.

Tears were snatched from her eyes by the wind. Her ears filled with the sounds of the wind rushing by at mach speed and the screech of sled runners slicing through snow and ice. In what seemed like no more than a few heartbeats she felt a bump and a slight slowing, and then another sharp drop as the sled swooped onto and then over the wide path and on down the hill.

She was just starting to get over the terror and beginning to enjoy herself when she heard Corbett yell in her ear, "We're coming to the road! Lean when I tell you!"

She nodded. A moment later she felt the sled begin to tip to one side. "Lean!"

This she was only too happy to do. Every instinct in her brain was telling her body to throw itself in the direction opposite the way the sled was tipping in order to keep it upright. So that's what she did.

The next thing she knew, the sled was slipping sideways down the hill, then skewing around and around, and she and the sled and Corbett were all cartwheeling, rolling, tumbling down the mountainside in a wild melee of flailing limbs and clouds of snow.

And then…all was still.

A few seconds passed before Lucia decided she was indeed alive. Shortly after that she decided she must be lying on her back, and since nothing seemed to hurt too terribly, all of her body parts must be intact and in working order. To test this theory, she spat out a mouthful of snow and attempted to sit up. And discovered she couldn't move.

Panic seized her—for the few seconds it took her to figure out that she was not paralyzed, but that something heavy was lying on top of her, and that the something, or someone, was Corbett.

"Kindly…don't do that…." His strangled whisper came from somewhere near her ear.

"Do what?"

"Move."

"Oh." There was a pause, and then: "Oh! Oh, my God! Corbett—your ribs—are you all right?"

"Not really, no. Though it wouldn't be quite so bad if you'd only stop wiggling."

"Oh. Sorry." She let her head drop back into the snow. Then popped it up again. "It's your own fault, you know. You told me to lean."

"Of course I did." Corbett's face loomed above hers, eyebrows and lashes woolly with snow, cheeks chafed and wet with it. He'd lost the fur hat, and his hair hung damply onto his forehead. "Dammit, I wanted to turn."

"Well, I leaned, and look what happened!"

"You leaned the wrong way, you…you— You shot the bloody sled right out from under us."

"How was I supposed to know?" She propped herself on her elbows, bringing her face almost nose to nose with his. "It felt like the sled was going to tip over. Call me crazy, but that seemed like a bad thing to me. So I leaned the other way to keep it from doing that!"

"What? Didn't you take physics in high school? Don't you ever watch the Olympics? There's this thing called centrifugal force—"

"It would have been nice if you'd explained that to me before you put me on that…that death sled! I told you I was no good at sports, but did you listen to me? Hell, n—mmf…"

He'd stood it as long as he could, he really had. Lying there with her body pinned beneath him, even with his wretched ribs on fire, had been enough of a torment. Then, to have that mouth of hers, the mouth he'd tried hard not to watch or think about for so many years only to have it invade his dreams and slip into his waking mind when he least expected it…to have that mouth right there, so close to his, red and swollen, wet and cold… Well.

And there was the added plus that it was a great way to get her to be still.

He kissed her.

Forcefully, at first, just to cut off the tirade. Forcefully enough so that he felt those lips stop moving and go still with shock, then quiver and begin to warm and soften against his. He drew back, then—not far, just to see her reaction. Her eyes gazed up at him, glistening like liquid silver.

"Well, it's about time," she said huskily. "I was beginning to think—"

Before she could finish, Corbett lowered his mouth to take hers again, this time with all the tenderness and care he had in him, and all the longing he'd kept hidden and the joy he'd denied himself for so long.

He pulled his hand from where it had been entombed in the snow, leaving his glove behind, and laid his cold fingers against her cheek. He wiped the snow-melt moisture away and felt the velvety softness of her skin and put his mouth there, too. Then to the cold, pink tip of her nose, one quivering eyelid, and back to her mouth again. He both felt and heard her faint little sigh, and now when he drew back to look at her, he found her eyes closed, and teardrops shivering on the tips of her lashes.

"You don't know…" Her lips looked blurred and barely seemed to move.

"Yes," he said softly, "I do."

"No, you don't. I tried to tell you—"

So he kissed her again. And this time he felt her arms come around his neck and her body lift under him, and he heard a whimper of passion. He turned slightly to give her room, scarcely aware of discomforts in any part of his body, save one. And that was one discomfort he was willing to live with—for a while. He didn't even mind making it worse, temporarily, as when he let his hand wander along the side of her body, then around to the small of her back and over the taut rounds of her bottom, then pressed her, with her full cooperation, against the part of himself that was suffering the most.

Though he couldn't help but groan.

She heard him, of course, and, drawing the wrong conclusion, stiffened. But before she could pull away, he tightened his arm around her and pressed her even closer, and with her lips curving under his in a smile of understanding, felt her legs shift to make a nest for him.

And as he was rocking against the cradle she'd made for him, his body tensing and tightening in familiar ways, seeking a union impossible under those circumstances, it struck him. First, as frustrating and infuriating, then as ridiculous, and finally, as hilariously funny. He withdrew gently from her mouth and rested his forehead against hers, his body shaking with laughter.

"Ow," he moaned, and went on laughing.

"What?" she whispered, still holding him, but tensely now. "Did you hurt your ribs? What's funny?"

It was a moment before he could answer, in a voice choked with pain and a kind of mirth he hadn't known in a very long time. "This is— We are. Us."

It was all he could manage. How could he tell her he felt ashamed he'd ever thought himself too old for her, when here he was behaving—and even more remarkable, feeling—like a randy adolescent? How could he explain that the joy he felt at this moment of discovering her was inextricably entwined with sadness for having waited so long? And perhaps most complicated of all, how could any words capture the bitter irony in having such a thing happen to him now, when his life was in chaos and everything he'd worked to build about to topple around him.

He raised his head and looked down at her, smiling and cupping her face in his hand. "We really can't do this, you know. At least, not here."

She tilted her chin upward in a way he recognized and said fiercely, "Why not?"

He kissed her forehead, laughing silently. "Now who's crazy? For one thing, my dearest, we're on the side of a mountain, in full view of a public road. Oh, and there's the small fact that it's quite likely we'd freeze to death. You do realize we're lying in the snow?"

"Hmm," she said, "I hadn't noticed. Though now that you mention it, I'm surprised we haven't melted it for quite some distance around." Then they were both laughing, holding each other and shaking helplessly with it.

When the laughter had died away into fitful murmurs and sighs and an occasional plaintive, "Ow," Corbett kissed her once more, then said gruffly, "We do have to get up. I'm sorry…"

Her eyes were closed, the long, thick lashes stuck together in spiky clumps. There was a long pause, and then instead of answering she clamped a hand over her eyes. Her mouth had a crushed look that made him hurt inside.

"What is it?" he whispered. "What's wrong?"

She shook her head and he thought she wouldn't answer. Then a single sob escaped her before she quickly gulped it back.

He took her hand and pulled it away from her face. "Open your eyes…look at me. Now…tell me."

Those remarkable eyes gazed back at him…silver blue ringed with indigo. And he knew before she said the words.

"Oh, Corbett, I don't want to let you go. I'm afraid…"

"Afraid?"

Oh, she was, she was. She stared up into his face—now wearing a stern expression she'd come to know and dread—and trembling, began to speak rapidly, trying to say everything before he stopped her.

"Of letting you go. Of letting this go—this moment. Afraid you'll back away again. That you'll step back behind your boss-teacher-mentor barrier the way you've always done when we've almost…when we've gotten…close. And then act as if nothing happened."

There. And he hadn't stopped her.

For a long suspenseful moment he went on looking at her, while even her heartbeat seemed to slow down. Then he rolled carefully away from her. Deep within her the pain began, and cold sickness flooded through her body. She'd known this would happen. Known he would do this.

Holding one arm protectively across his ribs, he pushed himself to his feet, then reached down to give her his hand. Too weak-kneed and shaky to rise on her own, Lucia took it gratefully.

Just let me survive this, she thought. *If I do, I'm leaving, I swear. I'm leaving the Lazlo Group, and I'm never coming back.*

And then, somehow, miraculously, warm arms and a hard, strong body were enfolding her. Cold fingers tipped her chin upward and warm lips brushed hers.

"I think we've pretty much gone beyond the point of no return, don't you?" Corbett said softly.

A tiny cry was all that escaped her before his mouth opened in perfect sync with hers, and her head fell back and her mind shut down.

As he deepened the kiss, then deepened it some

more, he felt Lucia—whose mind he'd held in awe, whose charm and beauty had enthralled him and whose strength and courage had saved his life—melt in his arms in complete and total surrender. Joy spread through him, and in his mind was one triumphant thought:

So...even brilliant minds go silent in awe of miracles.

Chapter 9

The point of no return...

Ordinarily, those words had an ominous ring. Today, Lucia couldn't think of any more beautiful. A lovely quietness settled over her, carrying with it the knowledge that there was no more urgency, that she had time to say to him all she wanted to say, ask all she wanted to ask. This was the man she would love for the rest of her life. *Be with* for the rest of her life. They would have all the time in the world.

She was happy. So it didn't occur to her, not then, that she might be wrong.

She murmured a gentle protest, and when he withdrew enough, she let her lips curve against his. "Then let's go in," she whispered, loving the way their mouths touched. "I want to have a look at your ribs. I hope we didn't—"

"I want to have a look at your ribs, as well," he said in a husky growl. "Among other things."

And she gave a gasp of sheer delight at the playfulness of it. She'd never experienced Corbett's sense of humor personally. How many times had she listened from a distance while he exchanged droll banter with other people—Adam, for instance—wishing with all her heart he could relax and be himself with her? And now... Laughing, she rested her head for a moment against his shoulder, then slipped an arm around his waist.

"You've lost your hat," she said, gazing up at him. "And one of your gloves."

"And you have snow in your hair," he countered, brushing at it tenderly. He paused, looking around. "I know where the glove is, I think. Ah, yes—here it is." He bent down to retrieve the glove from the snow, brushed it off and stuffed it into the pocket of his coat. "I don't feel much like climbing back up that mountain to look for a hat, though, do you?"

Holding his eyes with hers, she shook her head. "I think there are more important things we should be doing."

"Such as?"

She bit down on her lower lip to stop the shivers of anticipation already coursing through her body and said somberly, "We're both chilled through to the bone. I think we should both take a bath so we don't catch cold. A nice...hot...bath."

He gave her a startled look, then laughed out loud. "God," he said, as he snaked an arm around her and pulled her close to his side, "how I do love a smart woman."

They separated at the cottage's front gate, Corbett to return the sled to Josef's woodshed, Lucia to brush as much snow and mud from her clothes as she could, then tiptoe alone through the empty house like a cat burglar. She was glad not to have to greet Josef and Kati, certain her newfound happiness must be written all over her in neon lights.

In the passageway between the cottage and the cave house, she stopped to take off her boots and unzip her jacket, shook the last of the snow out of it and pulled the cap from her head. Then she opened the door and slipped into the kitchen.

And found it warm and bright and dense with a multitude of cooking smells, and Kati bustling between the sink and the table, where Josef sat placidly smoking an old-fashioned curved and handpainted pipe. Both greeted Lucia with a cheerful Magyar duet in soprano and baritone, Kati waving a soup ladle, Josef his pipe, to which Lucia responded with a breathless smile, hoping her dismay didn't show.

Kati clucked and scolded over Lucia's wet hair and clothes and refused to understand her clumsy efforts to explain how they'd gotten that way, while Josef watched with bright, shrewd eyes from behind a wreath of smoke. A moment later when Corbett came in, red-cheeked and grinning, with his clothes in much the same shape, both lobbed a barrage of questions at him, Kati's staccato rising over Josef's steady bass accompaniment.

Corbett rattled off a reply, then looked over at Lucia…and winked. She didn't have to know the exact translation; heat rose in her cheeks as two pairs of inquisitive eyes darted her way, and the duet rose once more in knowing "oohs" and "ahhs" and delighted laughter. She was about to flee to her room with as much dignity as she could manage, when Corbett took her gently by the arms.

"You might as well get used to it, *édesem,*" he said softly as he guided her to a chair, pulled it out and sat her down. "The cat's out of the bag, and no great surprise to them, either. Kati's been after me to 'find someone and settle down' for years. Evidently, she decided the minute she laid eyes on you that you were the one."

"Smart woman," Lucia murmured shakily, smiling across the table at Kati, who beamed back at her.

"I seem to be surrounded with them," Corbett said cheerfully. "Quite outnumbered, in fact."

"Oh, please, what's that song?" Lucia nodded toward Kati, who was now busily stirring something on the stove, both the stirring and the bobbing of her ample behind keeping time with the happy little tune she was singing. "She was singing the same song the first morning we were here. I heard it when I woke up. It stuck in my head, and I meant to ask you—"

"Ah—just a minute. I'll ask. *Kérem szépen...*"

At Corbett's query, Kati turned from the stove expectantly. There was a brief but spirited exchange between them, then she and Josef began to sing together with great enthusiasm:

"Kis kút kerekes kút van az udvarunkba
Egy szép barna kislány van a szomszédunkba
Csalfa szemeimet rá sem merem vetni
Fiatal az édesanyja azt is kell szeretni."

Lucia listened avidly and thought it interesting that, while neither of them could be said to have particularly good voices, together they sounded wonderful.

"Okay," Corbett said when they'd finished, while Lucia was still applauding, "I think I've got most of it. It's quite an old song. Kati says her mother used to sing it to my father when she was his nanny. It goes, 'There is a small well in our yard… There is a pretty brown girl in our neighborhood. I don't dare to give her the eye…' Dah dah dah dah—*Fiatal az édesanyja*—something about her having a young mother who needs love, too."

"That darn age thing—it'll get you every time," Lucia said solemnly.

His eyes smiled deeply into hers. She'd never seen them so blue and bright. "Yes, well, I think where Kati's concerned, the pertinent phrase is, 'Pretty little brown girl.' I must say, I find it appropriate, myself, if a bit inadequate."

And just that easily the room and everything in it disappeared—everything but him…his voice…his eyes. Nothing else mattered. Nothing else existed. She didn't care who knew, or what anyone might see in her eyes, her face. Just that quickly her world, her existence had come down to this: this man and the miracle that he loved her at last, the way she had always loved him.

And at that moment she was so happy, she hadn't the sense to be terrified.

The midday meal went on and on, as it always did, while Corbett clung to his legendary self-control like a drowning man to a bit of flotsam. It did no good whatsoever to tell himself how absurd it was for a man his age to be in such a state. Neither did it help to remind himself that in the room next door to this one a very sophisticated communications system sat waiting to connect him at the

click of a mouse to the agency he'd built and the responsibilities he'd abdicated. That people he cared about
might at this very moment be wounded or dying, that one
of those people had betrayed him and that the son he
hadn't known existed was lying paralyzed in a hospital.

All it did was make him feel guilty. Guilty because
all he wanted to do at this moment was get to a quiet
place where he could be alone with Lucia. Where he
could explore bit by tantalizing bit the miracle that this
woman who had loved him for so very long had reached
so far into his heart that he was able to truly love her the
same way. Where he could discover the mysteries of her
body and her heart at the same time she was discovering his.

He'd waited long enough. *Too* long, but that was the
past.

This was *now*. And since he had no way of knowing
whether they would have a future, he meant to make the
most of it.

Eventually, the last morsel of pastry had been offered
and regretfully refused, the last cup of coffee poured
and drunk, the last tiny glass of sweet *tokai* wine lifted
in toast and swiftly downed. When Josef seemed about
to relight his pipe and settle in for more conversation, his
wife, with silent scoldings and meaningful looks toward
the two younger people at the table, nudged him toward
the door.

And suddenly they were alone.

In the silence, Corbett looked at Lucia and smiled—
he thought a bit crookedly. She returned his gaze
steadily, though a sweet pink blush rose to her cheeks
as he watched. And his heart turned over.

"Still feel like that bath?" he asked, the huskiness in his voice the only outward sign of the strange new vulnerability that had come over him.

"I thought you'd never ask," she murmured in reply. She pushed back her chair and reached for his hand.

He took it and held it for a moment, fighting the urge to pull her into his lap, weighing the immediacy of the pleasures that activity promised, versus the delay it would cause to his ultimate goal. As a compromise, he rose to his feet, drew her close and folded his arms around her. She nestled against him with a sigh and her arms came carefully to circle his waist.

"Are you sure?" she whispered, tilting her head back to look at him. "What about your ribs?"

He kissed her forehead. "Hmm. Sweet of you to ask. It may require some creativity on both our parts, but with your brains and my…shall we say…motivation, I'm sure we'll manage."

"*Your* motivation? What about mine? Do you know how long I've wanted—"

"My fault entirely. As I believe you pointed out to me the other day, I have been a complete idiot. I believe I may be cured of that malady, but if I should ever begin to show signs of relapse, please feel free to pummel me soundly about the—"

At that point, mercifully, she muttered, "Oh, *do* shut up," hooked one hand around the back of his neck, pulled his head down and kissed him. Soundly.

When she released him some time later, he lifted his head, managed to pull her face into focus and said sternly, "Is that any way to speak to your—"

So she kissed him again.

This time when he'd recovered his senses somewhat, he had presence of mind to place a restraining finger across her lips before he attempted to speak. "As enjoyable as this is, my love, I have to ask…are you stalling? Because if you are—"

Above his hand her eyes grew wide and bright, and her head moved rapidly back and forth.

"In that case," he said, kissing her on the tip of her nose, "go and fetch us some towels and whatever else you need. And don't dawdle." He took her firmly by the shoulders and turned her toward her bedroom.

She went but paused in the doorway to give him a look over one shoulder. "Hmm. I can see there are one or two old habits in this relationship that will have to be dealt with," she said thoughtfully.

With the memory of Corbett's chuckle filling her whole being with happiness, Lucia quickly gathered an armful of towels, clean clothes, soap, lotion and shampoo. But, when she returned to the kitchen, she found him standing in the doorway of his study. He had his back to her, and something about the set of his shoulders—as if he bore the weight of a hundred sorrows on them—made her heart drop sickeningly into the pit of her stomach.

He didn't turn when she went to him, but silently reached an arm around her to pull her close.

"Corbett," she said softly, "if you want to check in first…"

He shook his head. A smile flickered briefly as he dropped a kiss on the top of her head. "No, love. It will all be here when I get to it. There's nothing I can do anyway, is there?"

He pulled the door closed, and they turned together to the one next to it.

Corbett took the lantern from its hook on the wall of the storage room, lit it, then turned off the overhead lights. The absolute darkness of the cave moved closer, but instead of seeming mysterious and even creepy, it seemed to embrace them in quiet intimacy. He led the way, lifting the lantern high so Lucia could see to pick her way through the maze of rock formations, and as she followed him deeper into the cave she seemed to slip deeper and deeper into a sense of unreality.

This is Corbett Lazlo.

Whenever she could, she studied the man walking ahead of her, watched the way he moved, as he always did, with confidence and grace, his head held high, and everything about him—his height, the breadth of his shoulders, his aristocratic bearing—bespeaking power and authority. He seemed larger than life, which she supposed was only natural for a man who had become a legend in his field.

The legendary Corbett Lazlo.

Funny, she thought, that in all the years she'd worked for him, and for all that time secretly been in love with him, she'd never once felt he might be beyond her reach. Infuriating, yes, for refusing to recognize she was a grown woman, intelligent and independent and capable of making her own choices, and not just his very young student and protégée, but never unattainable. Why now, when she'd finally won from him the things she'd longed for—both recognition and love—did she feel such overwhelming *awe?*

Corbett Lazlo, this amazing man, loves me.

Was that it? Was it the mere fact of being loved back by the man she'd chosen that filled her with such a profound sense of wonder? *Would this moment be as magical, would this feeling of being in a dream be the same if we were about to make love in his bed, or mine?*

"Wait here, love." Corbett's voice broke into her thoughts without scattering them.

She waited, leaning against the same stalactite—or stalagmite?—from which she'd startled him the day before, and watched him skirt the edge of the thermal pool. Watched him through a mist of wonder, rocking slightly from the pulsing of her heartbeat against the barrier of solid rock.

He placed the lantern on the ledge where it had sat that day, then came back to take her hand. "Watch your step—it can be slippery." He guided her around the edge of the pool to a wider spot where the rocks had formed a natural bench. "We can put our things here," he said, taking the armful of towels and toiletries from her and placing them on the bench. "Our clothes, too…if you like."

She nodded. And then, to her dismay, she shivered.

"Oops, sorry," she said, giving him a rueful smile, "I guess I'm a little nervous."

He took her hands, enfolded them in both of his and lifted them to his lips. "Believe it or not," he said huskily, "so am I."

She stared at him, studying the planes and hollows of his face as if she'd never seen them before as she said slowly, "I've seen you in nothing but a pair of shorts. You've seen me in my workout clothes. But this…it's different, isn't it?"

He kissed the backs of her fingers and gravely nodded. "It's different."

"I want you to see me, and I want to see you, but I…" She closed her eyes and caught a breath that felt sharp inside. "This is going to sound funny, since I've made such a point of telling you you're not my teacher, but—" she opened her eyes and tried again to smile "—I'd really like it if right now you'd tell me what to do."

"Hmm, okay…" He cocked his head and gave her one of his endearingly crooked smiles. "We may need to have a discussion at some point in the near future about the inference to be taken from that, but for the moment, glad to oblige. So here's what you do. Take these lovely hands, here, which, by the way, I believe are almost as cold as mine—"

"Oh—sorry!"

"Never mind," he said, tightening his hold when she tried to pull them away, "I fully intend to warm them soon enough. Anyway, as I was saying, you take these hands and place them here." He guided her hands to his waist as he spoke, and she uncurled them and felt the muscles of his torso grow taut against her palms. "Yes, that's lovely. Cold, but lovely. Now—"

But she was already gathering in the fabric of his pullover and tugging it free, lifting it and laying her hands on the smooth warm skin beneath. He caught a breath, then let it go in a sigh. "Ah, yes…that's it. How I do love a woman with a brilliant—" His breath hissed sharply between his teeth as she lifted the shirt higher and ducked her head to brush her mouth across his newly bared chest. She didn't flinch or gasp at the rainbow of colors spreading across the injured side of his chest, or the way his ribcage moved slightly out of sync when he breathed. It was only a part of him, of the man who was now a part of her, and perhaps a reminder to them both to go gently.

After that he may have spoken, but she didn't hear him, having lost herself in exploring the wonders of his body. His beautiful body, that she'd seen before—this part, at least—and imagined so often. But she could never have imagined the way it would make her feel to touch it like this…touch with her lips the textures of it, somehow both silky-smooth yet altogether masculine…taste with her tongue the salty tang of his skin, and know for the first time the raw, blood-stirring scent of a clean, healthy man's passion. She couldn't have imagined, as she touched him this way, that her own body would swell and tingle and lose all track of its own boundaries, as if she'd already began the process of ceasing to be one individual and becoming part of another. Becoming part of *him*—this man.

She couldn't have known how frightening it would be.

But then she felt his hands on her neck…her shoulders. Felt the power in them, and the gentleness. Fear fled. Though she couldn't have put any of it into words—either the reasons for the fear or the conquering of it—she somehow knew it was right, this coming together, this *oneness*. It was right because *he* was right. Right for her. Her heart had always known it, and now her soul and body knew it, too.

This is Corbett Lazlo, my love. Mine.

Joy and pride surged through her as his hands gathered her sweater and drew it over her head. She lifted her head and smiled at him as she pulled her arms free and he tossed the sweater onto the ledge. A moment later his pullover followed. She rested her fingertips on the uninjured side of his chest and gazed into his eyes. His eyes smiled back into hers as his searching fingers found the fastening on her bra. She gave a little hiccup of laughter as he drew the straps over her shoulders, then added the lacy scrap to the pile on the rock ledge.

Her nipples were already hard, so hard they hurt. Anticipating his touch made her tremble. His fingers, his mouth…either would be too intense. How would she stand it? Her legs were so weak already….

Then his hands were warm on her shoulders, stroking so lightly down her back, as if she were a wildcat to be gentled, guiding her toward him, bringing her against him so delicately, so softly she felt him first as a warm breath on her nipples, then a feather's touch, then the soft tickle of his hair. From there her sensitized nerves spread tingling heat throughout her body, making every part of her swell, and yearn…and she gasped out a sob of sheer relief when he brought her at last, oh, so gently, against him.

He folded his arms around her and her head came to snuggle into the hollow of his shoulder. He let his cheek rest on the soft, fragrant pillow of her curls and whispered brokenly, "You don't know how long I've wanted to do that. How good you feel."

"I don't think I want to know," she replied with a shaken sigh. "Because if it's any better than I feel right now I don't think I could stand it."

There were any number of thoughts that flashed through his mind, then. Things he might say in reply to that, things a confident, even arrogant man might have said. He'd been called both those things and probably deservedly, but he doubted anyone would believe him or understand if he tried to explain the way he felt right now. He didn't understand it himself. This strange vulnerability that came over him at odd moments—sometimes the worst possible moments—contrasted with a fierce protectiveness, the feeling he would find himself possessed of the strength of Hercules if that was what was needed to keep her safe. Intense pride that this woman— so young and bright and beautiful—was his, but also a humbling sense of awe that she should have chosen to be.

One thing he did know. He meant to spend the rest of his life trying very hard to see that she never regretted her choice.

All this went through his mind in the second or two it took him to reconnect with the fact that Lucia was shivering. He doubted it was entirely due to nerves, although she must have thought it was, since she seemed to be trying hard not to. It wasn't freezing cold in the cave, but it wasn't all that warm, either.

"Édesem," he said gently, "as lovely as this feels, the fact is, it's much warmer in the water. Do you mind if we proceed?"

She drew back, her hands slipping once more to his waist, and looked at him gravely. "No. I'd like it very much. What comes next?"

"Shoes," he said, after a moment's consideration. "Definitely. Otherwise removing one's trousers can quite easily become an exercise in low comedy."

She gave a snuffle of laughter, stifled it, then glared sternly at him long enough to say, "Yes, we certainly wouldn't want *comedy* intruding upon something as serious as sex." Then she gave in to the laughter once more. "Oh, dear," she said contritely when the giggles had subsided, "I am sorry. But I just realized how silly I'm being. As if we were the first two people ever to do this…"

"No, but it is the first time for *us* ever to do this. I think that warrants a certain degree of solemnity. Here—sit down and let's have a go at those boots. I am a patient man, my dear, but I'm discovering limits I didn't know I had." In the process of easing himself carefully onto one knee, he glanced up to see her gazing at him with widened eyes. "Oh, good heavens, don't look so alarmed. It's not so bad that I'm in danger of ravishing you—not just yet, anyway."

"Who said I was alarmed?" she said demurely, biting down on her lower lip in a way that made his mouth water.

Swiftly disposing of her ski boots, he hooked one hand around her neck, gathered a handful of her hair and brought her mouth to his. "I can see it's been entirely too long since I kissed you," he said, and did so, thoroughly, pulling her away from him only when his head began to swim and his heart to pound at a truly astonishing pace.

"Stand up," he growled, and she did without hesitation. He wondered if she felt the same urgency he did. Silently, she gripped his shoulders while he unzipped her pants and shucked them off of her, and when he wrapped his arms around her hips and lay his cheek against her belly, she only whimpered softly and cradled him closer, trembling a little. He turned his face to her and kissed her tight, satiny skin, and felt it quiver against his tongue.

Wishing he had more time…more patience…more

willpower, he rose slowly, kissed his way upward over her stomach, held her slender waist between his two hands and measured the urgency in her breathing, traced the sweet under-curve of each breast, and, in pausing to taste each tender tip, made her gasp sharply as if she'd felt pain. He straightened all the way, cradling her neck in one hand and trapping her leaping pulse in his mouth, with the other hand rapidly unbuckled his belt and unzipped his pants. He felt her hands touch his, then, and gratefully left the rest to her.

And there was nothing even remotely comedic in the graceful way she divested him of both pants and shoes.

Before rising, she did to him as he'd done to her— whether out of feminine mischief or innocent passion he would never know and never ask—wrapped her arms around his hips and lay her face against his belly. She briefly cradled the hot, hard length of him next to her body, then sweetly kissed him there, making him inhale sharply with something akin to pain. Then she rose swiftly, sliding her body the entire length of his until she joined her mouth with his in a hot, deep, drugging kiss.

He wondered—much later, when he could think again—if that was the precise moment when he, Corbett Lazlo, knew beyond any shadow of doubt that in Lucia Cordez he had more than met his match.

Chapter 10

They drew apart and turned at the same time, not abruptly, but like a well-tuned couple executing the steps of a dance. Corbett went first, wading into the thermal pool with sure-footed grace, while Lucia watched through a mist of love the way the lantern light played over the muscles in his back and buttocks and thighs. To her he seemed perfect, a classical statue in gleaming bronze come magically to life. She wanted to go to him, join him in that enchanted light, but suddenly it seemed too much, too overwhelming, too unbelievable. She felt the way she did in dreams sometimes, when her brain was telling her body to move and it just wouldn't obey.

Then he held out his hand. Hers went of its own accord to join with it, and at his firm, warm touch the dream fled. She was back in her own mind again, or a more primal form of it, empty of everything except her feminine response to his masculine call and a new and intense kind of joy, earthy and primitive as the ancients who had first taken shelter in these caves. He led her deeper into the pool, and she felt the steamy warmth envelope her like a sultry summer night.

In hip-deep water he drew her closer and, taking her head between his two hands, tilted her face to his and kissed her, a deep, lazy kiss that seemed to reach into her very soul, and she stood motionless, head back and eyes closed, and lost herself in it. Then, without breaking the kiss, he moved his hands slowly downward, over her shoulders, breasts and waist, and she followed his lead, both of them slicking the steam and sweat moisture over each other's skin like oil.

When their hands reached the place where buttocks swelled below the water's surface, he broke the kiss and his eyes looked into hers, a gaze like blue smoke. Smiling, eyes half-closed, she swayed toward him, sliding the soft places between her thighs over and around him in a playful, testing way. Though she felt his breathing cease and his hands tighten on her buttocks, he didn't rush or guide her, but held himself perfectly still and let her pleasure herself and him the way she wanted to. Until *she* could stand it no longer, and the pleasure became torment to her as it must have been to him.

"How deep is this pool?" she asked, slurring the words as if intoxicated.

"Not deep enough for this," he murmured. "But I think…"

Leading her by the hand and sliding his feet carefully on the slippery rock bottom, he moved them both a few steps closer to the edge of the pool. He eased himself down until he was lying in the water half-reclined, the way he'd been when she'd come upon him the day before, and when she followed him, her body seemed to slither over his and melt into perfect fit as if that was where it was always meant to be.

For all the chattering they'd done before, neither of them spoke a word now, save for the inarticulate moans and murmurs, the joyous little chuckles and sighs that were, perhaps, a language unto themselves. A language they each understood perfectly. She didn't have to tell him to go slowly, gently with her. He already knew, better than she did. He might have told her he'd never known a woman so sweetly in tune with him, but since she seemed to anticipate his every move, he thought it likely she knew his mind before he did.

Wherever his mouth and hands and fingers roamed, no matter how boldly, she welcomed his touch with passionate cries and sensual little wiggles of pleasure, responses that would have been reward enough, even if her hands and mouth hadn't wandered just as freely, and with an adventurousness that delighted him. She had no inhibitions with him, and so it was easy for him to let go of his own—except for those necessary limits he was reminded of now and then with a sharp stab of pain in his ribs, and those he grew accustomed to and could easily dismiss. He'd never felt so carefree. This woman—Lucia—she filled his senses *and* his mind as no woman ever had, so that for these blessed moments he could forget the worries and responsibilities that waited for him just beyond the cave.

A few blessed moments…

All too soon, there came the moment when he knew he'd waited as long as he could. And again he found that with her no words were necessary.

She sensed the new tension in his body and in his hands, in the fingers that had pleasured her with such cleverness and delicacy and that now gripped her thighs and urged them apart with urgency and purpose. She felt his body demanding entry into hers, and something— a primitive feminine instinct similar to fear—kicked beneath her ribs. She gasped, and even as she braced her hands on the rocky edge of the pool and gave herself up to his guidance, sought reassurance in his eyes.

His eyes shimmered back at her, bright with love and passion, as he whispered, "It's all right, *édesem…*" *My sweet*. And she knew it was.

He pushed against her barriers and her body relaxed its vigilance, let him in and invited him deeper with the small undulations and pulsations of welcome. Her legs straddled him, and the water gave them its buoyancy so that she was able to bring her legs completely around him, then rocked them gently while his hands held her still…held himself deeply seated in the place she'd made for him.

She looked into his eyes again, and the feelings inside her were so intense, tears sprang into hers. She closed them and wanted to explain, but no words would come and a sob rushed through her instead.

"I know," she heard him whisper. "I know. Come to me, love, let me kiss you."

She leaned down, her body quaking like a broken puppet's, and felt his hands come to hold her head and bring her mouth home. His fingers combed through her damp hair as his breath and essence merged with hers, and his body began to move in a way that was both old and new, a way that rocked her most nerve-rich places against his, and the sensations that shot through her were so bright and sharp they were almost like pain. She couldn't breathe, couldn't think, lost all track of her body and of time and space. Nothing existed for her but that terrible sensation and the pressure it was building inside her. She was sure she couldn't bear it—and just as sure she would die if it stopped.

And then inside her, under her, all around her Corbett's body seemed to grow bigger, stronger, more powerful, and she felt as if she were being lifted higher and higher, her body no longer hers to control. She tore her mouth from his and gave a single cry of panic as forces she'd never imagined seemed about to hurl her into oblivion. Except now it was that same body, Corbett's body, that held her, that caught her and cradled her in safety and kept her from falling, and his voice that crooned and comforted with words she didn't know but nevertheless understood. Words that meant love…only love. Always…love.

Slowly, her shaking stopped. And as all the parts of her came drifting back from the far corners of the cosmos and fitted themselves into their proper places, she began to be aware of other things, as well. Such as the fact that Corbett had turned them slightly to their sides, so she wasn't, as was her immediate fear, lying against his injured ribs. And although he hadn't withdrawn from her body completely, their legs were now entwined in a different and much more relaxed way. She felt entirely comfortable lying where she was. In fact, she never wanted to move from that place, with her ear resting right over the rapid but steady thumping of Corbett's heart.

After a while, afraid she might actually doze off, Lucia found the energy to murmur sleepily, *"La petite mort…"*

"'The little death'?" Corbett's voice and chuckle were gravelly. "Why do you say that, my love?"

"I've heard it's what the French call *orgasm*. Although I've never heard them say it myself."

She felt his lips graze her temple, felt them form a smile. "Hmm…what interesting bits of flotsam you have floating around in this pretty head of yours."

"It did seem something like that. Not that I know what dying is like…" She snuggled closer to him, loving the way his arm tightened around her, almost instinctively, it seemed. "But it was pretty overwhelming. Frightening, even. I've never felt anything like that before."

His body tensed and his head lifted. "You don't mean to tell me that was your first…"

"Well…no, not technically. I'm not *quite* a virgin." She paused, but he didn't say anything, so she went on. "I did some experimenting, when I first got to college. It was so nice not to be automatically labeled a nerd, I guess. It didn't last long, once I discovered that although I liked the attention, I didn't much care for the sex. I thought it highly overrated, if you want to know the truth." Finally becoming uneasy with his silence, she tilted her head back to look at him. "Should I not be talking about this? You're being awfully quiet."

He laughed softly. "There's nothing you can't talk

about with me, my love. It's just that every time I begin to think I know you, you find some new way to astonish me." He paused, then asked in a carefully neutral voice, "What about after college?"

"I met you," she said.

"Come now—you can't mean to tell me you've been celibate for ten years. You've been living in Paris. I know you've dated now and then. I know, because I considered having any man you went out with shot. Thought about it quite seriously, in fact."

She giggled, then kissed the underside of his jaw. "That's very sweet of you, dear. But quite unnecessary." The water rippled with her shrug, and she added softly, "I just found it impossible to make love with one man when I was madly in love with another."

He was silent for a long time, letting his hand glide slowly up and down her body. Then he stirred restlessly and muttered, "How could I have been such a bloody fool?"

She rolled onto her stomach, floating free, now, of his embrace. "Don't say that. I mean, okay, I thought that, too, for quite a long time, before I knew about… But now I wonder…" She paused, suddenly aware of how hard it was going to be to put her new perspective into words, and how dumb it could sound if she didn't get it right.

"Yes?" Corbett prompted, frowning, an edge of his old imperiousness creeping into his voice. "Wonder what?"

Knowing his impatience wasn't with her, she smiled crookedly. "There's a song called 'Somewhere'—I think it's from *West Side Story*—about 'a time and place for us.' Corbett, I think maybe *this* is it for us—the right time. Our time. I mean, before, there was Cassandra. The terrible way things ended between you, the way you felt about it—"

"You mean, the guilt," he said dryly.

She nodded, searching his face, trying to find the Corbett who'd just made such unforgettable love to her. Finding him in the eyes that pleaded with her for understanding. "I don't think you could have let yourself love me, then. You had to deal with her first."

His mouth spasmed briefly, as if he'd felt a sharp pain. "I haven't dealt with her yet, have I?"

"No, but the wound is open. It can heal, now. It's begun already."

He touched her shoulder lightly so that she floated closer to him, and he was completely *her* Corbett again. His smile made her ache. "If it has, you know, you're the one responsible. And, though it's sweet of you to acquit me, I still think I've been a bloody idiot."

With one finger touching just under her chin, he floated her closer still and kissed her a long, lazy time…a kiss so light and delicate at first she held herself utterly still, as if it were something magical, something that would vanish if she so much as breathed…then slowly, slowly deepened, became a different sort of enchantment, like a drug she craved with every ounce of her being. By the time he let her go she already felt a clenching deep down low in her belly, and the parts of her still swollen and sensitized from his earlier attentions had begun to throb.

"Nem szabad, édesem," he murmured, smiling tenderly. "As much as I would like to stay here with you

awhile longer, we are both beginning to prune. If we don't get ourselves out of this pond soon…"

"We may both discover what the other will look like when we're very, very old," Lucia said with a shiver. "And since I would very much like you to stick around that long…" She kissed him quickly and levered herself onto the edge of the pool.

She heard him say, "You may count on that," as he followed in a somewhat more complicated and cautious manner. He came to join her at the rock bench where she was toweling herself dry and trying not to think about the future at all.

She turned to him, and he took the ends of the towel in his hands and used it like a net to bring her close without touching her. She lay a hand, lightly as a breath, over the bruises on his torso and looked into his eyes. A tiny smile flicked at the corners of his mouth, but he didn't say anything, and she knew he was as reluctant as she was to burst the bubble. He released the towel and folded her into his arms, and with a grateful sigh she lay her head on his shoulder and let his musky heat warm her body as his whispered, *"Édesem…"* nourished her soul.

The world and all its uncertainties could wait just a little while longer.

Corbett left Lucia at the bedroom door and went on to the cottage to change into clean clothes. He was grateful not to encounter either of his old friends—it was choir practice night for Kati, and Josef would be working late in his shop, this close to Christmas. He couldn't have said why, but he didn't feel up to sharing the feelings he was certain he must be wearing, bald and naked on his face. Not yet. And Kati and Josef had eyes like hawks, particularly since they'd had matchmaking on their minds since the moment he and Lucia had arrived. And not all that subtly, either.

"Egy szép barna kislány…"

Little brown girl, indeed!

He was humming the tune under his breath when he walked back into the cave-house kitchen and found Lucia standing in the doorway of his study, waiting for him. One look at her face wiped every trace of music from his mind.

"Problems?" he said as he crossed the room to her, keeping his voice calm and his movements unhurried.

Her brow furrowed with a puzzled frown. "I'm not sure. I mean, it could be nothing, I suppose."

He thought, *Yes, and tomorrow the earth will turn out to be flat, after all.* "Tell me," he said softly.

"I can't raise Adam." She turned and made her way back to the bank of monitors. "It's possible the server's down, but the weird thing is, I can't seem to raise *anybody*."

"What do you mean, you can't raise *anybody?*" He was frowning, now, too. What she was saying to him didn't make sense. The Lazlo Group's communications system was a complex network involving literally hundreds of servers and thousands of connections worldwide. And nobody knew the system better than Lucia. After all, she was the one who'd set it up. "Explain."

"Corbett, I can't explain it. I've tried every way I can think of to establish a connection. Every single time I get the same message: 'Client Not Available.' I don't understand it. I keep thinking it must be something simple, so simple I'm overlooking it." Her eyes were bright with frustration.

She reminded him of a child with a toy that wouldn't work the way it was supposed to. And if the implications hadn't been so unthinkable, he might have found it amusing to see his beloved computer wizard in such an unheard-of state. *Almost.*

"Let's wait a bit, then have another go at it," he said. "It probably is something simple. Who knows, maybe it's a malfunction here, on our end."

"I don't—"

He kissed her lightly, enough to stop her denial, not quite enough to distract either of them *too* much. "I could do with a cup of coffee. How about you? Are you hungry?"

She shook her head. "Coffee sounds good, though." But she stole a look back at the monitors as she followed him into the kitchen, and the expression on her face left Corbett with a cold, sick feeling in the pit of his stomach.

Neither of them spoke while he was making the coffee, setting out cups, spoons, cream and sugar, but he could almost hear Lucia's mind ticking away as she sat staring at nothing. Every now and then he saw her give her head a little shake of vexation. He knew she was working on the problem like a dog with a particularly challenging bit of bone.

When he had filled their cups and returned the coffeepot to the stove, he pulled out a chair and sat down, deliberately choosing a spot across the table from her, far enough away so he wouldn't be able to touch her. Wrapping his hands around the steaming mug instead, he said gently, "Lu…love. Can you come back to me now?"

She gave a small start and her face took on a guilty look that made him smile. "Oh—yes, of course. I'm sorry, I was…"

"I know. But the problem's not going anywhere, unless it manages to figure out how to fix itself while we're on coffee break, in which case it's no longer a problem. Meanwhile, I need to ask you some questions. First, for the sake of discussion, let's assume our system *is* down. How could such a thing happen? Are we talking about hackers? Sabotage? What are we dealing with here?"

Lucia lifted her cup, set it back down and cleared her throat. "If by *sabotage* you mean physical damage to the equipment, I don't see how that would be possible—the system is spread out all over the world. I designed it to withstand almost anything short of the annihilation of the planet," she said, her cheeks showing heat. "There must be a thousand backup—"

"I know, my darling, I know. I guess by *sabotage* I mean more along the lines of viruses or hackers." His jaw clenched until he could feel his teeth grinding. "In other words, if the Lazlo Group system has been compromised, could Cassandra have done it?"

She looked at him with anguish in her eyes. He could see her throat working, knew how badly she didn't want to say the words. But he had to hear it from her. He had to. He didn't prod her or repeat the question. He simply waited. And after a long, tension-filled moment, she shook her head and said quietly, "No. Not without help. Security has been tight since Dani and Mitch caught Chloe selling us out. I saw it myself."

"From someone on the inside." He sat back, letting

out a long hissing breath. It was confirmation of what he'd already known. His eyes burned as he stared at Lucia. "How many people have the knowledge?"

"Corbett—"

"How many?"

"Adam," she said dully. "Me, of course. Your brother, Edward…"

He rubbed a hand over his eyes…wished he could rub out the thoughts behind them. "Anybody else?" *Please, tell me there's somebody else.*

"I—I don't know, I don't think so. Unless Adam or Edward told someone." She broke off to throw him a stricken look. "I meant—"

"Someone else in the agency—I know. Where are the access codes kept? Could anyone have got to them? From the outside?"

"No! Absolutely not. They're kept in the vault at headquarters. The security for that room is multiple biometrics, as you know. The only ones programmed for entry are you, me—"

"Adam and Edward. Yes…I know." He sat back in his chair, shifting his shoulders in a determined effort to ease the strain. "Then we will just have to hope for a simple explanation, won't we?"

Simple?

The bleak and unpleasant truth was that nothing in his life had been simple for a very long time. Thanks to the efforts over the past six months of some of his best agents, all too often at grave risk to their own lives, he'd become aware that there had to be a mole operating within the Lazlo Group. That had been hard enough to deal with when the list of possible suspects included every person in the agency, each and every one of whom he'd handpicked and trusted with his own life. But to have the field narrowed down to these three…

My brother, my best friend and the woman I love. Am I to believe one of them capable of betraying me to my worst enemy? My God.

He stared into his coffee cup, his heart tapping deep in his belly in a way he knew all too well. Dread… fear…the feeling went by any number of names, and he'd become familiar with it at other times when his life and future had hung in the balance. When the outcome had depended on people and events beyond his control. During one of the worst of those times, it had been Adam Sinclair who'd come through for him, at the cost of his own career. And there were all those times during his wild and misspent youth when he was certain the only thing standing between Corbett Lazlo and reform school had been his big brother, Edward—the *good* son. Which left…

Lucia.

He stole a look at her as he lifted his cup to his lips and sipped what had begun to taste as awful as battery acid to him. She was staring fixedly at her cup, her cheeks washed with pink—looking, quite frankly, guilty as hell. Which, in itself, meant nothing, of course; most innocent people did feel guilty when they knew they were being suspected of wrongdoing. A woman with her intelligence would quite likely know precisely what he was thinking. And he knew all too well what it was like to be the one all the evidence seemed to point to.

No. Not Lucia.

He could not—*would not*—believe this woman, this same woman he'd held in his arms such a short time ago, made love to until she'd sobbed and trembled in complete and total surrender, could betray him. He could not have been such a bloody awful fool. Could he?

Of course, there had been all those years when she'd been madly in love with him and he'd ignored her, dismissed her, flaunted other women in front of her. He cringed to think of all the times he'd stopped by her office on his way to or from a date, determined to prove something, he supposed—to her, to himself, who knows?—but an exercise in monumental stupidity however he sliced it.

And he did have a history of involving himself with women with a thirst for revenge….

Lucia?

Could she have been so angry at him at some point during those years as to let herself be persuaded—

No.

But that could be why she's feeling guilty about it now, and afraid to—

No, dammit. Not Lucia.

And what a complete jackass he was to let her sit there in guilty silence, thinking he was entertaining all sorts of doubts about her….

I've got to say something to him, Lucia thought. She'd held it in too long as it was. *I know he's thinking about it.* She could feel it pulsing like a living thing, as if another person were there in the room with them, standing between them.

"Corbett," she began, just as he said, "Lucia—"

They broke off together and then he was staring at her, frozen, his eyes like silver daggers.

"Go on," he said softly.

"No—that's all right, you—"

"Lucia."

Oh, God. She'd heard that tone of voice before. And she could see his jaw stiffening, see his body tensing, knew he was throwing up all his old barricades. This was going to be even harder than she'd imagined.

She drew a shuddering breath. "Corbett, there's something we have to talk about. I'm sorry, I know you don't—"

"Lucia, for God's sake!" His voice was like tearing cloth.

She held up a hand as if to deflect a blow, then snatched it back. "I know this is hard for you. Painful. And maybe you feel it isn't really my business, but—" She halted when he flinched back, as if she'd lobbed something at him instead.

"Not—your business?" And now, oddly, he seemed more confused than anything.

"Yes. I mean—" She closed her eyes and took another breath. Well, what could she do but blunder on? "This has all happened so suddenly. I think…I'm really not exactly sure what my status is—with you. But I do think this is important, to you and to both of us. So I have to ask. Corbett, you must have thought about it. What are you going to do about them? Cassandra. And…um…your son. What is his name? I'm not even sure…" She stumbled to a halt.

With all the responses she'd imagined, all the scenarios she'd played over in her mind, she hadn't expected this. Corbett had one hand over his eyes and was shaking with silent laughter.

She could only stare at him, wonder whether to be miffed and wait for an explanation. Which never really came, because after a moment he rubbed the hand over his face and said in a muffled voice, "Troy. I believe that's his name. My son…" Another spasm of inexplicable laughter rippled through him. He shook his head, then looked at her, eyes glistening with something that might have been grief or mirth, mixed with what looked bewilderingly like relief. As if the question she'd asked hadn't been nearly as hard for him as the one he'd been expecting.

He didn't give her a chance to mull that over, though, as he pushed back abruptly, rose and began to pace, raking his hair back with his fingers.

"You're quite right, you know. It *is* difficult for me to talk about. I don't know how to *feel* about it, for one thing. Guilt—a whole lot of that. Rage, sometimes. Sure, I'm angry. Mad as hell. More often, though— most of the time—I think what I feel is just…*sad.*" He paced a step or two without speaking, then threw Lucia a crooked smile. "What's weird, though, is that I have these moments where I actually feel this fierce kind of joy—purely instinctive, I suspect. Crikey, as Adam would say, I'm a dad! Am I crazy, or what? The kid wants to kill me. But, hey, he's my *son.*"

His lips twisted with a bitter little smile as he paused to grasp the back of a chair and lean his weight on it. "As for what I'm to do with him, given the fact that he is currently in police custody, I doubt I'll have much to say in the matter. If we'd been able to whisk him away before the authorities arrived, as we'd planned… But, as it is—"

"What about the fact that he *is* your son? Couldn't you say it was all a family quarrel gone wrong, some sort of misunderstanding, and given that the only real harm done was to the perpetrator, get the charges dismissed, or reduced, say, to something with probation or a suspended sentence?"

"You're forgetting," Corbett said dryly, "he's tried this a few times before."

"Yes, but the police don't know that. Do they? If you can keep him out of jail, maybe you could get him released into your custody…."

"He's nineteen years old, Lu. In criminal matters that's considered an adult in most countries. I do have a few connections, it's true…one or two favors I could probably call in. But there's the fact that we don't know who this boy is. We don't know how much damage his mother's managed to inflict on him. Considering he's got her genetic material and almost twenty years of her influence, for all we know the lad could be an unmitigated monster who absolutely belongs in jail."

"Yes, but he's got your genetic material, too. And you told me his mother wasn't always evil. And speaking of Cassandra, why haven't the police arrested her? Adam said she's been right there at her son's bedside ever since the shooting."

"And what would they charge her with? Just being a lousy mother isn't enough, I'm afraid."

"But Adam said she's the head of S.N.A.K.E. She must have been responsible for dozens of murders, drugs and weapons trafficking. What about that conflict-diamond business Witt uncovered last summer? Surely that—"

"And absolutely nothing can be traced back to her.

She's covered her tracks well, as you know. Even you weren't able to nail her as the source of those bloody e-mails that entertained us so nicely all summer and fall." He broke off, straightened and rubbed his hand over his eyes once more. "You know what the real irony is? This is precisely the sort of job the Lazlo Group would ordinarily take on. If I'd only caught on sooner to the possibility it was Cassandra behind it all, I believe we could have found the proof necessary to put the organization out of business and Cassandra behind bars for good. But as it is, I'm afraid she's got the drop on us, love. With the Group in complete disarray and no way to communicate—"

"Don't say that," Lucia said fiercely. "I've been running some diagnostics. Let me try again to reach Adam." *Or anyone else in the system,* she thought, as she pushed her chair back from the table. *Maybe even anyone* but *Adam…just in case.*

Ten minutes later she looked up from the bank of monitors and turned to face Corbett. Her heart felt like a chunk of hot lead in her chest, and she knew from the bleakness in his eyes that what she had to tell him was already written in hers.

"That's it, I'm sorry. The entire communications system is nonfunctional. It's been shut down, from headquarters to the most remote outpost. Everything. There's not a peep anywhere." She paused, then added in a voice that trembled, "It's as if the Lazlo Group has ceased to exist."

Chapter 11

"It's the only possible thing to do," Corbett said. "I have to go back immediately. You know that."

"Of course I know that," Lucia said with exaggerated patience, a ploy he thought was intended to keep her from falling apart completely, and which he could tell was only a good breath or two away from complete and utter failure. "What I do *not* understand is why you won't let me come with you."

"I've explained why," he said, in a manner that matched hers and, he was sure, was about to cause an inevitable flare-up of her temper. "I need you to stay here, try to access the Lazlo system, and ferret out our mole."

"Which I can do just as well on my laptop from anywhere on the planet," she shot back furiously, sitting up in bed and turning on him, evidently forgetting for the moment that she wasn't wearing any clothes. "Which you well know, *dammit*." The last word emerged with added emphasis as she snatched at the down comforter and jerked it up to cover her breasts.

In spite of the ache of sadness that seemed a permanent part of him now, he had to quell an urge to smile. Given her present state of mind, he didn't like to think what she might do if she thought he was laughing at her. Which was the farthest thing from his mind.

What *was* on his mind was trying to recall exactly how they'd come to be engaged in discussion at all, instead of the vastly more enjoyable activities they'd both had in mind when they'd reached the mutual conclusion that he should spend the night in his own bed—with her. But somehow, between the blood-stirring embraces in the kitchen and the unavoidable processes involved in retiring for the night—the teeth-brushing and the like— Lucia had asked him about, or he *might* have mentioned, his plans for the following day.

"*Édesem...*" He reached across her to hook a forefinger over the comforter where it draped between her breasts. Half expecting her to bat his hand away, he pulled it down to uncover her nipples. Finding them pertly erect in spite of the comforter's cozy warmth, he smiled. "I do know that. The truth is, I don't want you anywhere near Cassandra until she's been neutralized. In fact," he added fervently, "if I could find a way to send you off-planet, I would. She's vowed to kill you, you know. And I believe she means it."

"But you said it yourself," Lucia said, looking at him along her shoulder, her mouth set in a stubborn pout he was sure she had no idea made it look more delectable than determined. "It's you she really wants."

"I believe I'm a bit more able to look after myself than you are."

Oh, the confident smile, the lazy arrogance in his half-closed eyes… Even though Lucia knew what he said was true, and even though she knew the smile and the arrogance had more to do with what his hand was doing to her than what he'd said, she couldn't resist twisting around to stare pointedly at the fading bruises on his torso and murmuring, "Oh, yes, I can see that. What if—"

"Lucia," he interrupted in a stern, warning tone, without causing the slightest interruption in the slow sensual way his thumb was circling the rigid tip of her breast. "Don't make me play the I'm-your-boss card."

She valiantly narrowed her eyes and swallowed before attempting to speak, but still, the words came out slurred. "You wouldn't."

"Oh, I think you know I would." She felt him shift behind her, felt the warm flow of his breath on her naked shoulder. "Since I can tell you're going to leave me no choice…" She felt his mouth move in clever ways that shivered her skin into goose bumps and made all the nerve-rich parts of her swell and sing shamelessly, and entirely against her will. "I'm making it an order." She tried to turn her face away, but with a single finger touched to the underside of her chin he brought it back so that his steel-dagger eyes could stab relentlessly into hers. "Lucia Cordez, you are to stay here and catch me a mole, whilst I return to Paris to see what has become of the agency formerly known as the Lazlo Group. That is a direct order."

He leaned slowly forward and touched his lips to hers. Warm and firm and satiny, they moved over hers with the skill of an artisan, and she closed her eyes and her mind and gave herself up to him, and knew in that terrifying moment that this man, Corbett Lazlo, was not only her boss and her lover, but also master of her heart and soul. *My love…when did you become everything in the world to me? Painter of my heart's dreams…maker of my soul's music…*

"You are not to follow me until I tell you it is safe to do so. Do I make myself clear?"

A shudder shook her and she opened her eyes, trying desperately and without success to free herself from the web of enchantment he'd woven around her. She wanted to be angry with him, fight with him, scream at him in fury, but instead, she wanted him to make love to her. And the worst of it was, she knew he knew it.

How had she let this happen? When had he become master of *all* her being? Master of her heart and soul—that was one thing. Master of her body? Well, okay, *some* of the time. When *she* allowed it. But master of her mind?

Never.

"Perfectly," she purred.

"Promise me." She could see the wariness in his eyes. The man really did know her too well. "Promise me, Lu. I want to hear you say it. You will stay here until I tell you it's safe."

"I promise." She whispered it, surprised by the ache that had come to her throat from out of nowhere, and even more by the tear that was making its way slowly down her cheek.

He kissed it away, then took her mouth so sweetly, so tenderly, she knew he'd misunderstood the reason for the tears. He couldn't know it was the lie, not the promise, that was breaking her heart.

"Don't cry, *édesem*," he said huskily. "It's going to be all right, you know. I just don't think I could bear it if anything happened to you. You've become part of me, you see. From now on, for the rest of my life, you are a very important part of me."

She touched her finger to his lips and in a choked voice, said, "Promise? I want to hear you say it...."

His smile was beauty itself. "Yes, love, I promise to love you dearly, cherish and protect you for the rest of my life. How's that?"

She couldn't answer, but only stifled her gathering sobs in his mouth. And she thought, *Will you still love me, my dearest one, when I've broken the very first promise I made to you?*

Corbett felt the shudders that racked her body and recognized them for the struggle they betrayed. He knew his Lucia very well, and knew what it had cost her to make him such a promise. And, to be completely honest with himself, he didn't entirely trust her to keep it.

Which was why before he left tomorrow he intended to make it very clear to Josef and Kati that they were to make absolutely certain she did.

For now, though, he was only glad the conflicts had been resolved to his satisfaction, and with the woman he adored softly, sweetly compliant in his arms. He still felt his lovemaking skills somewhat hampered by his injured ribs, but the tenderness he felt for her, and his gratitude for the way she'd given in, he hoped would make up for that.

The fact was, he'd never before made love in the grip

of such powerful emotions. He felt they'd changed him in ways he hadn't begun to understand yet, but which scared him a little. He knew for certain that when he left this house tomorrow he wouldn't be the same Corbett Lazlo he'd been when he'd arrived. What he didn't know was…would he be less strong because he had so much to lose? Or all the stronger for having so much to fight for?

For now, there was, thank God, Lucia. Only Lucia.

It confounded and amazed him how happy he was to be with her, touching her, kissing her, hearing her earthy little sounds of pleasure. Before Lucia, sex had been at best mildly enjoyable, on those occasions when he'd had needs of his own to be met, and at worst a chore that left him feeling soulless and depressed. Even with Cassandra, as wildly exciting as that liaison had been, there'd also been an element of fear, of danger, involving, at times, a good bit of adrenaline. He'd never gone to bed with her without feeling at least a smidgen of dread.

But Lucia…making love with her was complete and utter joy. He wondered if it might be because her love for him matched his for her, and that he didn't have to be anything other than who and what he was. He didn't have to think about what he was going to do, what way to touch her, what part of his body to put where. All he had to do was *feel,* and his body fit naturally with hers, and everywhere they came together there was only sweetness and pleasure.

He didn't have to wonder what might please her, or whether he was pleasing her. He knew his simply *being* pleased her, knew it because she told him with every breath she took. She told him with her shining, tear-filled eyes and kiss-swollen lips. Told him with the way her skin grew moist and dusky and her body trembled and writhed closer to him when his fingers gently stroked its tender places. Told him with the way she hesitated, at first, when he kissed her thighs and belly, asking her with his touch to let his mouth caress those tender places…then yielded to him with complete and total trust.

That trust and the way she opened her body to him touched him deeply. He felt it more intensely than any pain, as if she'd opened his heart and physically touched him there. Penetrating that most intimate part of her body with his tongue seemed to him a sort of parallel to what she was doing to the most intimate part of his being. And when, as he kissed her deeply, then more deeply still, he heard her sharp cry, and while he held her close with his mouth and hands through her body's shuddering, throbbing release, he felt the echoes of those same responses swell through him like a tsunami after an earthquake.

In its aftermath he held her in his arms and comforted her while she sobbed, and she held him tightly, too. And he wondered who needed the comforting more.

He'd gladly have held her like that until she fell asleep, but she wouldn't hear of that, especially when her wandering hands found him hard and hot and in some discomfort still. She wouldn't let him take it slowly for her sake, either, but quickly, firmly guided him, kneeling, between her thighs. As she opened her body to him, her eyes and lips smiled up at him, lush reminders of the welcome waiting for him there.

And so, whispering her name in awe and love, he

pushed himself between her still moist, still swollen folds and felt her softness give way to him and her warmth envelop him. Felt her hands stroking him… belly, buttocks, thighs. Felt them press the aching place in the small of his back, press it hard there, urging him deeper, deeper…then releasing the pressure as her body moved in perfect sync with his.

All too soon, he felt her hands grasp and hold him tightly as the spasms caught him and his muscles clenched so fiercely they seemed to be trying to turn him inside out. And in the midst of that cataclysm he heard her whispering over and over the words he'd said so often to her:

"Édesem…édesem…"

It was sometime deep in the night, after he'd kissed his restless love and told her again to sleep, that it came to him, the reason why he couldn't seem to follow his own advice, and instead lay wide-awake with a sense of dread lying cold and heavy on his heart.

He'd made a terrible mistake.

Lucia loved him. Loved him the way she did everything, wholeheartedly, completely, passionately. And, dammit, the devil take her promises—she was never going to let him go alone to face Cassandra! He knew her too well. Lioness that she was, and having already convinced herself—admittedly with some good reason—that she'd saved his life once, she would find a way to be at his side, or at least his back, during the next confrontation. That clever and agile mind of hers had probably already figured out a dozen ways to thwart whatever plan he might come up with to prevent her from following him back to Paris.

In the bleakest, coldest hours of the night it came to him. He knew there was one way, and probably *only* one way, to undo his mistake. One way he *might* convince her to stay here, where she'd be safe. And that was to break her heart.

Corbett was gone when Lucia woke up. She knew before she opened her eyes that there was only emptiness where his warm body had been, silence instead of the deep, masculine breathing that had found its way into the rhythm of her sleep. Only his scent remained, and she gathered the pillow that held it into her arms and pressed her face to it and tried to make the pain inside her stop.

He's gone.

She curled herself into a ball around Corbett's pillow while the battle between anger and misery raged within her, tearing her throat with dry, tearless sobs and tying her stomach in knots.

She'd known he'd try to slip away without disturbing her, and she'd tried so hard to stay awake. Several times she'd jerked herself out of a doze to find his arms still around her and heard him whisper, "Shh, *édesem,* go back to sleep."

And so she had, and he'd left her without saying goodbye.

As she lay wrapped in her ball of misery, she heard a clatter from the kitchen—most uncharacteristic of Kati, who somehow managed her culinary miracles with a minimum of disturbance, save for her singing. Lucia sat bolt upright in bed, adrenaline shivering through her body, heartbeat thumping. *Maybe he hasn't gone yet. He must still be here, in the kitchen, having his breakfast, his coffee. I can still catch him!*

She scrambled out of bed and tore through her suitcase, snatching up items of clothing without regard to type or style. Somehow, jangled and shaking, desperate to think Corbett would finish his coffee and leave and she'd have missed him by only seconds, she managed to throw on a pair of jeans and a soft-knit pullover—sans underwear. Barefooted and breathless, she threw open the kitchen door.

He was there, not relaxing at the table with his coffee, as she'd imagined, but rinsing his plate and cup at the sink—the source of the clattering crockery that had alerted her. He turned at the sound of the opening door to look at her.

And several realizations hit her in the blink of an eye:

His face had registered no surprise or chagrin at seeing her there.

Of course! He can move like a cat when he wants to. He made that noise on purpose, to wake me.

But there was no leap of joy in her heart. She'd already seen his eyes.

Something's wrong. Something's very, very wrong.

Fear with neither name nor shape crawled coldly along the back of her neck.

Corbett watched her face, saw her skin go from sleep-flushed to gray, noted the way her taut nipples pushed against the soft material of her shirt and the way she folded her arms protectively across them. She was sensitive, as well as brilliant. Of course she already knew *something* was wrong. She'd sensed it the way a doe senses danger.

"Sorry I woke you," he said with a small, tight smile, steeling himself for what had to be. "I meant—"

"—to steal away like a thief in the night—I know." She came to him and lifted her face for his kiss. "Why is that, I wonder?"

"Why, indeed," he said dryly. He kissed her with lips that didn't soften—however much they wanted to— then gripped her arms and put her firmly from him. "Perhaps because I knew you'd try to persuade me to let you come along. You *are* going to try, aren't you?"

"Well, yes, but Corbett—"

"*Lucia.*" He closed his eyes and ran a weary hand over them. "We've been through all this. I don't want you—"

"Corbett, I won't be a liability. I think I've proven that I can handle myself in a crisis situation. I know you think—"

"Good God, Lucia, you have no idea what I think!" He spun away from her, in part because he couldn't bear to see the flush of earnestness on her cheeks, the fire in her eyes, in part because he couldn't let her see the anguish in his.

When he had himself in hand again, he said coldly, "The fact is, I don't want you in this fight with me. Do you understand?"

"No, I don't." But she said it faintly, and he could see she was beginning to.

He swore under his breath. Raked a hand through his hair. "Look—Lucia. I don't want to hurt you. I really don't." He paused, then let it go in an angry rush. "You really are going to make me say this, aren't you? Dammit, I can't let you back me up in this fight, because…hell, the truth is, I don't know if I can trust you."

She stood absolutely still, head slightly tilted, as if straining to hear some faraway sound. The silence between them rang in Corbett's ears like a clamoring of bells.

After what seemed like whole minutes had passed, she whispered, "You think *I'm* the mole?"

He had to grip the back of a chair and pray for the strength to finish, looking her straight in her hurt-filled eyes. "My dear, you are one of three people in the world it could possibly be."

She gave her head a disbelieving shake. "But…last night—"

"Ah—yes. Last night." He smiled crookedly. "Last night I may not have been thinking clearly—certainly not with my brain, at any rate. In the clear light of day it's simply not possible to ignore the fact that there are only three people with means, opportunity and know-how to feed information to Cassandra. And of those three, I've known both Edward and Adam a whole lot longer than I have you." He shrugged and wondered whether his expression looked as sick as he felt. "Sorry, love. But until I know for certain, I'd rather not have you along when push comes to shove. Do you understand?"

She opened her mouth, cleared her throat and, finally, incapable of speech, simply nodded.

"Good. All right then. I'll be off." He pushed himself away from the chair that had been his anchor and support and moved jerkily to the door. He didn't kiss her…couldn't bear to touch her. He took his coat and hat from their hooks near the door and half turned, not quite looking at her. "You won't be able to contact me,

so just sit tight until you hear from me—understand?"
He didn't wait to hear her reply.

In the passageway he paused to take deep breaths and
swear softly and vehemently at the ceiling in two languages. For a few insane moments he was bitterly angry,
not with himself, as would have been well-deserved
and reasonable, but with *her.* With Lucia. Damned
quick, she'd been, to swallow the whole load of lies.
Had she so little belief in him? Did his words of love
mean nothing to her, that she could think him capable
of being such an unmitigated cad?

But then...he closed his eyes and let out a long
breath. Of course. It was too new, this thing between
them. Too fragile and untried. She'd be full of wonder
and uncertainty, as he was.

And it hit him then—the worst thing about the terrible lies he'd spoken to her was that maybe they
weren't lies at all. That maybe, just maybe, deep down
inside, he did have his doubts about Lucia even now.

They hadn't yet learned to trust each other. He wondered whether...he hoped and prayed...they still could.

Lucia's knees buckled and she sank heavily into a
fortuitously placed chair. For a long time she felt nothing. Not sorrow, grief or even outrage. Just...nothing.

Then gradually, like a rumbling beginning far away
and moving steadily closer, closer, she could hear
words, words that grew louder and louder until they
were a thunder inside her head she could no longer
ignore.

Find me a mole.
It isn't me. It isn't me. It isn't me.

That was the only thing that was real to her now. She knew she was not the person betraying Corbett and the Lazlo Group. Gradually, with that thought as her anchor and her starting point, her mind began to function again.

And with its function came emotions. Anger. *Pain.* Anger again—yes, that was better. She could work with anger.

Okay, if Corbett wanted a mole, by God, she'd find it for him. And hand it to him on a silver plate. Personally. Even if the truth broke his heart. Or hers.

Adam or Edward? She knew it wasn't her, and it wasn't Corbett, so it had to be one of those two.

She couldn't believe it of Adam. He'd been Corbett's best friend since their days in British intelligence, and it had been Adam who'd worked so hard and sacrificed his own career to clear Corbett when he'd been framed for treason. He'd helped to found the Lazlo Group. It seemed inconceivable that he'd now want to destroy it along with the man who'd been like a brother to him.

But then…how well did she really know Adam Sinclair? A person's circumstances could change. Maybe he had reasons she didn't know about.

Then there was Edward Lazlo, Corbett's own brother. A bit of a bounder, it was true, but still loved and in a strange way looked up to by his younger and much more worthy brother. In an even stranger way, she realized Corbett felt responsible for his brother, which was why he'd made him controller for the Lazlo Group. It would devastate Corbett to learn his own brother had conspired with his worst enemy to destroy him.

Edward or Adam?

Either way, it wouldn't be good news for Corbett.

Lucia sat quietly, her mind working feverishly to map out her plan of attack. One phrase kept creeping into her thoughts, one she'd heard many times before— admittedly, mostly in movies and television dramas, but it did seem to make a certain amount of sense. *Follow the money.*

Yes, she thought, *that might just be the fastest way to the truth.*

She was still sitting there an unknown amount of time later when Kati came in, muttering sorrowfully over Corbett's absence, to prepare her breakfast.

Corbett found it fitting that, as he drove down from the mountains of northern Hungary to the Danube River valley, he should leave behind clear skies and a brilliant moon casting its winter enchantment over a landscape lying peacefully under a fresh dusting of snow, only to have the coming of daylight reveal a dismal gray-and-brown world and a sun reluctant to emerge from behind a pall of dirty fog. He felt every bit as gray and dismal and was no more eager than that surly red sun for the task that lay ahead of him.

He had plenty of time during the drive to Salzburg to contemplate what that change of heart meant to his life and his future. He'd expected his feelings for Lucia to have changed him, of course, but he hadn't expected to discover he'd completely lost his taste for his chosen profession.

Although, when he thought about it more, it wasn't really his work with the Lazlo Group he dreaded. That work had given him considerable satisfaction—not to mention financial reward—over the years, and he'd made a good many lasting friendships because of it, both among the agents he'd employed and worked with, and the clients he'd served so well. He'd have been more than happy if that was what he had to look forward to today.

However, the Lazlo Group was currently in a shambles, and most of his best people in hiding—too many others dead or missing in action. Add to that the fact that he was about to face down the woman responsible, who also happened to be the woman he'd once treated abominably, plus the son who hated him so much he'd tried three times to kill him.

Then there was the other person he had to face—the one who'd stabbed him in the back. He had plenty of time on that long drive to think about *that,* as well, and doing so left him with no conclusions and a gnawing ache in his belly.

Not Lucia. She's too open, too honest. I've worked side by side with her, taught her everything I know, and I've always known she had feelings for me, I just didn't want to let myself believe they were real. Maybe didn't believe I had a right to her love...who knows? But I know she's not capable of betraying me. And certainly not without my knowing. It's not Lucia.

Not Edward. He's my brother. More to the point, he'd have way too much to lose by destroying the Lazlo Group—it's the only thing keeping him financially afloat, most of the time. Although, I suppose...if someone made him a better offer.... No, he's my brother, dammit! It's not Edward.

Not Adam. He's been my best friend for more than half my life, the one person I could count on to watch my back when it counted. He's saved my life a dozen times. Why would he betray me now? For the sake of a woman? Is it possible that because of Lucia... No, dammit, I know him! It's not Adam.

But it had to be one of the three, didn't it? He'd been over it a thousand times, looking for a loophole in that conclusion. And there wasn't one.

The gnawing pain in his belly was joined by a pounding one in his head.

He thought again of Lucia and the dawning realization that his life was half over and there was a whole part of it he'd missed out on. The part that included a home filled with warmth and children and love. And not having to go through life all alone.

He thought of Edward. Even as greedy and vain as he could be, he had a family, nice wife, kids, though he probably didn't know the real value of them. Edward's son, Josh, for instance. A great kid, who'd grown into a fine man and one of Corbett's best agents. And now about to marry the prime minister's daughter. From all accounts Prudence Hill could be a bit of a handful, but Corbett knew if anybody could deal with a bright and feisty woman, it was his nephew.

Thinking of that made Corbett smile. It had been one of the bright spots in an otherwise trying time.

Although, when he thought about it, there had been others, these past six months, Lazlo Group agents past, present and future, who'd somehow managed to find new love—or rediscover an old one—in the midst of the chaos and mayhem all around them. Mitch and Dani, back from the dead. Witt and British SIS agent, Marina Bond. The return of Sean McGregor to the fold, and his reunion with his former wife, Natalie—another British intelligence agent. And just last month, perhaps most surprising of all, Mark Alexander and that American undercover agent, Renee Sabine…

Food for thought, certainly. Corbett hadn't quite got to the point where he was picturing himself puttering around in a rose garden or building model trains in the basement, but he was beginning to wonder whether it might be possible after all to have all those things he'd been missing—wife, kids, family—and still run the most respected private-security agency in the world. It would depend, he supposed, on the outcome of his current mission.

And whether Lucia would ever forgive him.

It turned out to be even easier than Lucia had thought it would be, finding the proof. Of course, it wasn't the first time she'd been called upon to access confidential financial records, but in this case there'd been a determined effort to hide the ill-gotten gains, and she was quite proud of the way she'd managed to untangle the web of deception and follow it to its sad conclusion.

It wasn't going to be easy for Corbett to hear this. Nor was it going to be easy for her to tell him, even if it did mean her own vindication.

After she'd transferred the incriminating records to a flash drive, she sat for a long time gazing at the monitor, chewing on her lip and wrestling with her choices. Corbett had made it abundantly clear he didn't trust her. If she disobeyed his orders—and broke her own promise, even if it was one she'd had every intention at the time of breaking—wouldn't she simply be proving him right? What if he decided he could never trust her again?

What if—the very thought made her feel cold and sick—she lost him forever?

On the other hand, she knew he'd want to have this information immediately, no matter how heartbreaking he was sure to find it. But she had no way to reach *him* and no choice but to sit here and twiddle her thumbs and go quietly mad until he decided to contact *her.*

And in the meantime he was going into what could be a life-or-death confrontation, and what if he chose the wrong person to trust?

She could still lose him forever.

It really was intolerable. And, she told herself, Corbett had been wrong not to trust her. Wrong to ask her to do something so unfair and unreasonable. Anger rose up in her and spilled over in the tears she'd been keeping bottled up. *Damn him! Why didn't he trust me? How could he think I would ever betray him? He doesn't know me at all! And if that's the case, what hope is there for us?*

Having convinced herself she had nothing to lose, Lucia wasted no time. She scrubbed away her tears with her shirt sleeve, popped the drive out of the computer, zipped it into a weatherproof pouch and left the study, fully intending to go straight to her room, gather up a few essentials and her cold-weather clothes and slip quietly out of the house. Once past the gate, she reasoned, she would make her way to the village, where she would knock on doors until she found someone with a telephone. And sufficient knowledge of English to be able to help her make transportation arrangements as far as Budapest. From there she would take a commercial flight to Paris. Piece of cake. She could be there by…well, either very late tonight, or at the latest, first thing tomorrow.

The only thing was, in order to get from the study to her room, she had to pass through the kitchen. And in the kitchen she found Kati, seated comfortably at the kitchen table as if she'd grown roots there, diligently working away on a piece of embroidery. She looked up when Lucia came in, her round, kind face registering dismay at the obvious evidence of her recent weeping. She immediately put down her sewing and bustled to Lucia's side, patting her shoulder and cooing her concern in animated Hungarian, inquiring whether Lucia would like some coffee? Some wine? Some cake? Lunch? Food and drink—the cure for all ills.

Lucia smiled tremulously, shook her head, waved Kati back to her work and went into the bedroom, where she lowered herself onto the bed with a dejected exhalation. Escaping from her prison wasn't going to be as easy as she'd hoped. Clearly, Kati and Josef had been designated her keepers, and given their devotion to Corbett, Lucia was sure nothing short of knockout drops in their *tokai* or a bonk on the head with a bit of crockery was likely to induce them to abandon their posts. And, since she lacked both knockout drops and the stomach for violence—the premeditated kind, anyway—she would simply have to come up with something more… creative.

Creative…

Like…sewing or embroidery. Like needlepoint.

Rising swiftly, she went to her suitcase and took out the large, handwoven bag she used to carry her needlework. She turned it upside down and dumped out everything into her suitcase. Then she put back into the bag a sweater, a change of underwear, several pairs of warm socks, her gloves, some essential toiletries, her flashlight, her wallet with her driver's license, credit card and a few euros, the flash drive and, lastly, the needlepoint project she'd been working on before that fateful night, the evening that was to have been a fairytale date with Corbett to the British Embassy Christmas party. It seemed a lifetime ago.

She sat for a moment staring down at the piece, a chair seat cushion cover that was part of a set she'd been working on forever, it seemed, she supposed in the expectation she might someday have a set of chairs to put them on. Looking at it now, it struck her that it didn't fit at all with either her lifestyle or her personal taste, which meant it would ultimately end up where all her needlework projects did—hanging on the wall of some elderly relative or rolled up in her mother's cedar chest. But before it did, this one, at least, might serve a better purpose. She had only the beginnings of an idea of how she might escape her loving watchdogs, but she was sure the rest would come.

Her lips curved in a secret little smile as she placed the square of fabric neatly into the bag so that it covered the items already there. The plastic case containing scissors and needles she dropped in, as well. Who knows, she thought, they might come in handy as a weapon.

She hoped the shiver that rippled through her wasn't a premonition.

She closed the suitcase and picked up the bag, then stood in the middle of the room and looked around, going over everything again in her mind.

Shoes. She'd need the ski boots. Hopefully Kati wouldn't notice, or if she did, wouldn't think it odd that she'd chosen to wear them indoors. She sat down on the bed to change into the boots, and as she did, her reading glasses, there on the nightstand, caught her eye. She'd need them, too, of course, for the sewing. She slipped them on and stood up…and once again inspiration struck. Smiling another secret smile, she removed the glasses and put them in the sewing bag, pushing them way down to the bottom.

Yes, she thought, the pieces of her plan were coming together. It was going to depend on a lot of things going her way, but it just might work.

When Lucia returned to the kitchen, Kati beamed and nodded, and when she saw the needlework Lucia pulled out of her bag, gave a little crow of delight and hastily pushed her own things out of the way to make more room on the table. The other woman's obvious pleasure in having company during her assigned vigil made Lucia's stomach clench with regret.

I'll make it up to you, somehow, she silently promised as she bent over her sewing bag, making a great show out of searching for something and her consternation at not finding it.

When Kati asked what was wrong, making it clear from her eager expression that perhaps she could produce the missing item from her own supplies, Lucia shook her head and pointed to her own eyes with a perplexed frown.

"I can't find my glasses," she explained. "I know I left them… Oh—no, wait!" *Lord, forgive me, and please make me a good enough actress to pull this off….*

"I remember now. I think I left them in the cave yesterday, when I was, um…when Corbett and I were…I mean, when *I* was taking a bath." As she augmented her English explanation with elaborate pantomime she could feel a blush warming her cheeks. At least she didn't have to fake *that.* "I'll just…go…." She rose and gestured toward the storeroom door.

Kati nodded sagely and gave her a sideways look, eyes sparkling with the glee she didn't try very hard to hide.

Having made it as far as the storeroom, and with the door safely shut behind her, Lucia paused for a moment to lean against it and send up one last prayer for forgiveness. Then she dug her flashlight out of her sewing bag, drew a deep breath and ventured into the cool, damp darkness of the cave.

Lucia was fairly familiar with the path as far as the thermal pool. Beyond that, she'd be venturing into unknown territory. She had no way of knowing whether there would even be a path. She wished with all her heart she'd found a way to explore, maybe even find the chimney, before this. Now all she had was the flashlight and a very powerful incentive.

But as she paused beside the thermal pool, she felt shivers of apprehension and the first real shadows of doubt.

Am I doing the right thing? Will Corbett forgive me?

Even if he did forgive her for disobeying his order, he'd probably never forgive her—or Kati and Josef, either—if she got herself killed.

Nevertheless, it was vitally important that she get the information about the identity of the mole to him before he did something that couldn't be undone. For that, she knew, she'd never forgive herself.

She would simply have to make certain she didn't get herself killed.

It's no different from any other search. Use your head. Use your logic.

How had she tackled the search for the mole?

Follow the money.

In this case she was looking for a tunnel, a chimney that might be a way out of the cave. How had she known about the existence of such a thing in the first place? *Air currents.* She'd felt the breeze stirring through the cave. All she had to do was find that breeze again, then follow it.

Follow the current....

It wasn't that easy, of course. She'd never been a Girl Scout, and those wilderness trips with her parents hadn't included spelunking. But eventually she did find a spot where there seemed to be a breath of fresh air, apparently coming from an offshoot of the main cavern that appeared to be a dead end.

Her heart beat faster as she made her way into the smaller passageway, and it dropped into her stomach when the passage seemed to grow steadily smaller and narrower, and its ceiling lower, until she had to grope her way forward on her hands and knees, pushing the flashlight and her sewing bag ahead of her.

Nightmare scenarios kept her company in the darkness: *What if the chimney is no longer passable? What if its been blocked by a cave-in or rock slide?*

If that did turn out to be the case, the worst that could happen would be that she'd have to turn back, and either try to find another way to slip past Kati and Josef or convince them to let her go. Since neither of those seemed a very likely alternative, she pressed on, although she was conscious, now, of the unknown tons of earth and rock pressing down on the ceiling above her. Having allowed the notion of cave-ins and rock falls to invade her thoughts, she'd let fear creep in with it. Fear that turned her skin clammy and her knees weak. A sudden attack of paralyzing claustrophobia seemed like a real possibility.

The only thing that kept her from giving in to panic completely was the realization that the air current did seem to be getting stronger. The chimney *must* be up ahead, somewhere. And getting closer.

And then she came to the end of the passageway.

Close to despair, she directed the flashlight all around the walls, searching for a seam, a crack of some kind. Finding nothing, she pounded her hand against the smooth walls in frustration. How could this be? The breeze…

The breeze was gone. She didn't feel it anymore. When had it disappeared?

Creeping backward, she directed the light toward the ceiling. And a few yards back she found it—an opening big enough for a man to stand upright in. In her frightened focus on moving ahead she'd gone right past it.

She stood up shakily and aimed the flashlight's beam higher into the hole. *There*—she could see where rusted iron spikes had been driven at intervals into the rock walls of the chimney. The first seemed too high to reach, but she discovered that by standing on her tiptoes she could just get a hand round it. It seemed solid enough. If only the others were, as well.

Now…how to hoist herself up into the chimney? She was no monkey; her upper-body strength wouldn't be nearly up to the task. The problem had her stumped, until a search found shallow toe-holes carved in the tunnel walls directly below the shaft.

Thankful now for the height that had seemed such a burden to her in her gangly, geeky youth, Lucia tucked her flashlight into the waistband of her ski pants, looped the handles of her sewing bag securely over one shoulder and began to climb.

Chapter 12

Corbett set the Lazlo Group's unmarked Citation down on a private and little-known airstrip in the countryside near Paris in a sullen gray overcast that perfectly matched his mood. He found the airfield deserted, the hangars and small terminal building locked up tight. This didn't surprise him—given the state of the Group's communications system, he'd feared something of the sort and had called ahead from Salzburg. When he'd gotten no answer at the airfield, he'd arranged for a cab to meet him. He could see the car now, the only one in the small graveled parking lot, engine off, the driver dozing behind the wheel.

He taxied the Citation into the shelter next to the larger of the two hangars, chocked its wheels, then jog-trotted around the terminal office building to the parking lot. When he tapped on the cabdriver's window, the fellow jerked upright with a wide grin and spoke to him with a French accent Corbett thought might be Algerian. Corbett gave him a small salute, and the driver stretched an arm around to unlock the back door. Corbett opened it, tossed in his kit bag and climbed in after it.

Scarcely an hour later they were driving into the heart of Paris, just as night and a drizzly rain began to fall.

To Lucia's profound relief, the vertical section of the shaft was only about ten or fifteen feet high—enough, though, for her shoulder, arm and leg muscles to begin to tremble rather alarmingly by the time she reached the first bend. From there on it angled upward at an easier slant, though still steep enough that she had to brace herself with her feet against the sides of the shaft to keep from slipping backward—which she did once or twice anyway, terrifyingly, heart-stoppingly, each time losing two or three feet before managing to stop her slide.

Eventually, after some interesting twists and turns and narrow places and one more sharp climb, she emerged into a small chamber filled with rocks and debris. Realizing this must be where the original discoverers of the shaft had broken through while digging their cistern, Lucia was elated—until she realized the ceiling of the cavern was at least three feet beyond her reach. Furthermore, she couldn't see any signs of daylight, not a crack or a glimmer showing through at all.

Was this the end? Had the hole been filled in? Had she come this far only to have to turn back at this last stage before success—and freedom?

She sank to the floor of the chamber, exhausted and

defeated, every muscle in her body quivering with fatigue. The sweat that had dampened her hair and sweater during her strenuous climb now chilled her to the bone. She couldn't stay here long; she'd have to start back soon. But first…just a little rest. And in the meantime, she'd turn off the flashlight to save the batteries. She had no idea how long she'd been climbing, but even her long-life LED work light wouldn't hold out forever.

To keep the sudden blackness from being such a shock, she closed her eyes before switching off the flashlight. When she did, all the thoughts that fear and concentration had been holding at bay came flooding into her mind.

How long have I been gone?

Poor Kati—what must she have thought when I didn't come back? Have they been looking for me? Why haven't I heard them in the cave?

What will Corbett say when he hears what I've done? He'll be furious!

This was a stupid thing to do!

Oh, God, I hate to think about going back, creeping ignominiously back to face Kati's tears and Josef's… Well, he'll be angry, almost certainly, but worried, most of all.

I feel so bad about that—making them worry.

It's all such a mess. If only I could just stay here… sleep… just for a little while….

No! She couldn't do that. Hypothermia would take her for sure. She had to move, start back *now.*

She opened her eyes and lay staring up at the blackness overhead, willing her tired body to move. And that was when she saw it. A crack… Not light, exactly, just a lighter bit of the darkness, so faint she thought at first it was only a phantom of some sort, a flaw on her retinas. *But a straight line? What had Corbett said? Nature abhors a straight line....*

She stood up and turned on the flashlight, studying the ceiling intently where she thought she'd seen the crack. And now she could see what she'd missed before: the faint outline of a wooden trapdoor, so coated with the mossy moldy growth of years, it was barely distinguishable from the earth around it.

Elation surged through her, then ebbed as quickly when she remembered she still had no way to reach the trapdoor. She needed a ladder. There must have been one at one time, she reasoned. Maybe it was still here, buried under the rubble.

Propping her flashlight on her sewing bag, she dropped to her knees and began to push, shove and roll the bigger rocks toward the center of the chamber. If nothing else, she told herself, fired with new determination, maybe she could pile them high enough so she could reach the door that way.

She'd scraped a good bit of skin off her hands before she remembered the gloves she had stashed in her bag, and once she had them on, it wasn't long before her efforts hit paydirt. Along one wall she found a crude wooden ladder, where it had obviously fallen and remained undisturbed for years.

But again, her joy at the discovery was short-lived. The uprights, made of sturdy saplings, seemed strong enough, but several of the rungs had rotted away completely, and the ones that were left seemed unlikely to support her weight.

Furious, refusing to accept defeat now that victory was so close, Lucia snatched up her sewing bag and dumped the contents onto the dirt floor of the chamber. She had scissors. Underwear. Socks. A sweater. Enough material there, surely, to tie the rungs to the ladder. Scissors to cut the fabric into strips, and then to notch the wood.

Having made her decision, she wasted no time on second thoughts. Working quickly, she cut her bra, underpants, socks and—although it made her whimper to do it—her favorite pullover sweater into strips, then used the scissors to chip away groves in the rungs and uprights. She used only the soundest of the remaining rungs, spacing them far enough apart that they would enable her—she hoped and prayed—to climb high enough to open the trapdoor and pull herself through it.

She pulled the last knot tight, then quickly stuffed everything back into the now-lighter sewing bag and once again looped it over her shoulder. With scissors in hand and the flashlight in her waistband, she propped the makeshift ladder against the trapdoor's thick wooden frame set into the ceiling and, trying not to think about the reliability of her untested and unskilled handiwork, hauled herself cautiously, step by step, up the ladder.

At the top, as she'd feared, she found the trapdoor stuck tightly shut. But, after some diligent chipping and digging with the scissors, she felt it begin to give.

And so did the ladder.

She gave a squawk of panic and one final desperate shove with the points of the scissors. The trapdoor toppled over, away from the opening. She managed to grab hold of the frame with both hands and hoist herself over the edge, just as the ladder gave way under her feet and fell into the chamber below.

Half sobbing, half laughing, Lucia hauled herself onto the floor of the cistern Corbett had shown her just... How long had it been? Two days ago? Three? She'd lost track. And of the hours, as well. She understood, now, why she hadn't been able to see daylight through the crack in the trapdoor. She hadn't seen it, because there wasn't any. Days were short this close to winter solstice. While she had been working her way up the chimney shaft, night had fallen.

She rolled onto her back and lay still for a few minutes, resting. Looking up at the stars. More stars than she'd ever seen, except maybe for those long-ago camping trips in the High Sierras. She thought she'd never seen stars so beautiful, and she thought of Corbett, and the skylight above his bed, and his words:

"Having come much too near to losing the privilege forever, I do like to be able to see the stars."

Now, she understood.

In the quiet suburban neighborhood that surrounded the hospital complex, a taxicab rolled slowly and almost silently through wet streets that reflected the displays of Christmas lights in a cheery kaleidoscope of reds and greens. Few other cars were out and about, and those splashed briskly past on their holiday errands, paying no attention to the cruising cab.

On its third pass down a deserted side street a block or so from the well-lit hospital parking areas, Corbett leaned forward to speak to the taxi driver.

"Mon ami, je vous quitte ici. Merci, et pardon pour le dérangement."

The driver, who had been well paid already, protested volubly that it had been no trouble, and he would be more than happy to drop the gentleman someplace more hospitable. Corbett clapped him on the shoulder and pressed another wad of euros into his waiting hand. The driver gave an elaborate shrug and pulled to the curbside. Corbett opened the street-side door and stepped out into the steady drizzle. The driver muttered, *"Bonne chance, monsieur,"* and drove away.

When the taxi's taillights had winked out around the far corner, Corbett turned up the collar of his coat, put his hands in the pockets, hunched his shoulders and began to walk toward the car that was parked on the street a short distance away. It was an unremarkable car, dark in color, small, German-made, though not recently. Droplets of rain shimmered on the hood and on all the windows, making it impossible to see who was inside.

As Corbett approached the driver's side of the car, deep in his right coat pocket, his fingers flexed and tightened around the butt of a Walther P38.

He drew level with the window and it slid silently down. From the darkness inside came a voice with a familiar Australian accent.

"About time you showed up," Adam Sinclair said. "I was beginning to lose faith in you, mate."

Lucia stood in the ruins of the medieval castle, looking down on the rooftops of the village below. It couldn't be too late, she decided, since the streets and many of the houses were still showing lights.

That was the good news.

The bad news was, her plan to go knocking on doors until she found someone with a telephone she could borrow was probably not the best idea. By this time, Kati and Josef would have spread the word that she was missing. In a town so small, it was a sure bet everyone would have received the news by now.

Still, what other choice did she have? The night was clear and growing colder. She'd freeze to death if she didn't get down off this mountaintop and into someplace warm, and *soon.*

After studying the straight, snowy drop straight down to the village, she turned reluctantly to the winding path—the longer, but infinitely safer way down the hill. And vowed, as soon as possible after all this was over, to ask Corbett—assuming he was still speaking to her—to teach her to ski.

"Had no choice, Laz. We were being hacked. I had to shut down in a hurry." Adam stared straight ahead at the spangled windshield. His profile was grim.

"How far did they get?" Corbett asked in a flat voice.

"Far enough. I terminated all the ops we still had running, called in our agents and told 'em to go underground until they hear from you." In the dim light of the streetlamps, Adam's grin flashed at him briefly. "'Course, they didn't do any such thing. They're all here, cocked and ready, just say the word. Didn't have time to get word to you and Lucia, but I had an idea you'd be showing up here once you found out the whole system'd gone dark. I've been parked here since yesterday—well, in the neighborhood, anyway. Just in case."

Corbett allowed himself a wry smile. "How did you know I'd find you?"

"Truth is, I didn't. I've got our lads watching every way there is into that bloody hospital up there. Couldn't risk it myself—our S.N.A.K.E. charmer knows me on sight." He held up a cell phone. "I'm supposed to get a heads-up call if you show."

Corbett stared narrow-eyed at the lighted medical complex just ahead. "She's still there, then?"

"Hasn't left the boy's side since the shooting. She's got a bed in his room. So they tell me."

Corbett nodded, and after a moment felt Adam turn to look at him. "So. What's the plan?" Once again he waved the cell phone. "We're ready to move. Just say the word."

He'd had plenty of time to think about it, on the flight from Salzburg and on the taxi ride into the city. He knew what he had to do. What he didn't know was how much he dared tell Adam. How far he could trust him. He couldn't afford to guess wrong. Doubt sat in his stomach like a rock.

"Too late to do anything now," he said. "Prison wing will be locked down—I'm assuming that's where they've got him?" Adam nodded without speaking, watching him narrowly. "So since she's not going anywhere tonight, my immediate plan is to find a bed and a shower and something to eat. Not necessarily in that order. Got any suggestions?"

Adam grinned and reached for the ignition key. "I'm

way ahead of you, mate." Then, with the engine idling and the heater beginning to cough out chilly air, he paused and asked casually, "How's Lucia? Not too happy about being left behind, I guess."

"No, not happy," Corbett said with a dark smile. "But safe." He paused, then added, "Or…she will be, if she stays where I put her."

Adam gave a bark of laughter. "Good luck with that," he said as he put the car in gear.

Please, God, Corbett prayed bleakly, *let her stay where I put her. Please, let her obey me this once. If she just does it this one time, I'll never ask her to do such a thing again, I swear. Assuming we have more of that— time.*

Lucia wasn't quite sure whether to be glad or sorry to find no one abroad in the village's main street. At least she didn't have to worry about meeting anyone. But, if anyone *should* happen to pass by or glance out a window, she was bound to look a little odd. Hard to pass for one of the village lasses with her dark skin and wild Gypsy curls, particularly out and about alone on a cold December evening wearing dirty ski pants, boots, gloves and cap, but no jacket.

Then there was the problem of how she was going to find a telephone. Knocking on the door of someone's home seemed out of the question. But a gasthaus, perhaps…or a pub? She could explain that she'd had car trouble…a flat, maybe. Or run her car into a ditch. But, assuming someone didn't immediately phone Kati and Josef, or the local authorities, what then? Even if she could find a phone, who would she call? What transportation service would likely be available in such an out-of-the-way place at this time of night?

Not for the first time, she wondered if she would finally have to give up, go creeping shamefaced back to the cottage and beg forgiveness of the kind and caring people Corbett had charged with keeping her here.

And you, Corbett, my love. Where are you now? Fighting your battle…alone?

He'd gone back to Paris knowing only that someone he trusted had betrayed him. What if he went to the wrong person for help? What if he decided to trust no one and tried to tackle his enemies alone?

I can't quit now. I have to get to him. I can't let him do this alone!

And once more, just when despair seemed imminent, she lifted her eyes…and beheld salvation.

This time salvation came in the form of a panel truck, parked outside what appeared to be a bistro. Although the driver was nowhere to be seen, the truck's motor was running, feathery plumes of vapor waving from the exhaust pipe in a way that seemed almost friendly… hospitable, like the smoke from a cottage chimney in an otherwise deserted landscape. But what truly made it seem like a miracle to Lucia's tired eyes, a chariot straight from heaven, was what was painted on the side. In familiar red-and-white script were two words understood in any language:

Coca-Cola.

Without stopping to dwell on the unbelievably good luck, or question whether she should, she tried the truck's back door. She wasn't even surprised to find it unlocked. She crawled inside, closed the door securely behind her, and finding just enough room between the boxes of bottles and cans of syrup, lay down on the floor of the truck with the sewing bag under her head for a pillow.

She didn't mean to fall asleep. However, the next thing she knew she was being jolted awake by the clang of the truck's metal doors. Stiff, sore and completely disoriented, she lifted her head and blinked owlishly at the gray daylight, while a strange male voice shouted exclamations and questions at her in Hungarian.

Thanks to his numerous trips to America to visit his brother in Cincinnati—as he later explained to her—the truck driver's command of English was reasonably good. Thus, she was able to, firstly, convince him not to immediately summon the police, and secondly, discover that, yes, she was now on the outskirts of Budapest. Even better, not far from the airport.

So it was, that barely an hour after sunrise, thanks to a kind and America-friendly Coca-Cola delivery-truck driver and most of her small supply of euros, Lucia was walking into the main terminal at the Budapest airport. An hour or so after that, thanks to her Visa card, she was about to board the first flight of the day to Paris, dressed in a new pair of jeans, leather boots and a very cool-looking black leather jacket. And, just in case there was an international APB out on her, a yellow beret and dark glasses—also very cool.

She still had her sewing bag, although the inspectors at the security checkpoint had confiscated her scissors.

By midmorning Corbett Lazlo, wearing the coveralls and cloth cap of a member of the hospital's janitorial staff and pushing a mop, was making his way slowly along the corridor just outside the maximum-security wing.

It was a quiet time in the wards and corridors, relatively speaking. The doctors had made their rounds, medications had been dispensed, breakfast trays served and cleared away. It was too early for lunch and visitors were limited to members of a patient's immediate family. Most of the traffic Corbett encountered now consisted of patients, scheduled for various tests, procedures and therapies, being trundled off to labs and operating rooms.

It was not by chance that Corbett was in that particular place at that particular time.

Earlier that morning, by means of a focused flirtation with one of the nurses just going off her shift, and some promises he didn't intend to keep, he'd learned that there'd been quite a bit of interest, not to mention gossip, about the very good-looking young man in the jail wing, recovering from a gunshot wound and injury to the spine. It was said he'd attempted to assassinate someone famous. Speculation as to who that famous person might be ranged from Michael Jackson to the French president's mistress. Of much greater interest to Corbett, however, was the information that this young man was scheduled to receive his first physical-therapy session this morning at ten o'clock.

He was still some distance from the double sets of reinforced doors leading to the prison wing when a loud buzzer sounded. He paused to watch, leaning on his mop and wiping his face with a large handkerchief, while first one, then the other set of doors swung open

to allow passage of a hospital bed carrying a sullen-
looking young man encased in a full-body brace. The
bed was pushed along by a very large French West-
African orderly and accompanied by an armed uniformed police guard. Walking beside the bed, one hand
placed solicitously on the young man's shoulder, was a
tall, slender woman with red-gold hair. None of these
paid the slightest attention to the janitor as they passed.

Corbett waited until the caravan had turned the corner at the end of the hallway, then leaned the mop carefully against the wall, tucked the handkerchief into his
back pocket and sauntered after the group.

During his early morning reconnaissance he'd noted
and marked the presence of several suspiciously bulky
individuals in and around the hospital he felt fairly
certain were Cassandra DuMont's thugs. He spotted
two more now. He'd also identified three of his own
agents manning their posts at strategic locations around
the prison wing, but had not made himself known to
them. He did not do so now, either, primarily because
he didn't feel like explaining why he was operating
without his usual backup, any more than he wanted to
explain to Adam why he was choosing to take on Cassandra and her crew alone.

Adam would figure it out, of course, once he realized
the stakeout Corbett had assigned him was a red herring.
By the time he did, Corbett sincerely hoped *he* would
have everything figured out, as well.

Lucia was stuck in traffic. A pile-up on the rain-
slick freeway during morning rush hour had been
cleared, but by the time traffic was moving again it

was already midmorning. She was also hungry. She'd considered whether to take time to eat something before leaving the airport, but a persistent sense of urgency, not to mention a shortage of euros, had convinced her to head for the car-rental counter instead. The coffee and biscuits she'd eaten on the plane were now a distant memory.

The map and directions to the French hospital supplied to her by the rental-car agency proved accurate, and once clear of the traffic slowdown she made good time. It was a few minutes past ten when she pulled into the hospital's visitor parking area, only to find it full. With no time to waste driving around in circles, hoping to catch someone pulling out, she exited the lot with an angry screech of tires and, luckily, found a place to park on one of the side streets. Of course, the rear end of her rental car was partly blocking someone's driveway, but, she told herself, that couldn't be helped.

With the help of the car's rearview mirror, she put on her new beret, tucked all her hair up inside and adjusted it to a jaunty angle. Then she put on her new sunglasses—notably unnecessary in the December overcast—and got out of the car, locked it and pocketed the key. She left the sewing bag behind, having first removed from it a blunt knitting needle, which she'd inserted into the lining of her jacket just inside the right sleeve.

She made her way briskly along the wet sidewalk toward the hospital's main entrance, sparing only the briefest glance and a quick thank-you wave to the driver of the old black BMW who had stopped to let her cross the street.

* * *

At the wheel of the BMW, Adam Sinclair lifted
one finger in acknowledgment of the wave, then
turned his head to watch the woman jog up the
hospital steps. He did this purely as a reflex, a natural
male response to a tall, shapely woman with a confident and sexy walk.

An instant later the same car was screeching around
a corner and into the hospital's emergency loading zone.
Swearing as only an Aussie can, Adam opened the car
door and bolted for the sliding doors before the engine
had stopped running.

In the physical-therapy waiting area, Cassandra
DuMont sat leafing through a magazine with impatient,
jerky movements. No one else was around, the orderly
and police guard having disappeared down the hallway
and into one of the rooms in the large therapy complex
with their patient and prisoner. And the woman didn't
bother to give the man in the janitor's coveralls and cap
a second glance—until he sat down in one of the chairs
across from her.

She looked up, then, with hot, angry eyes poised,
Corbett was sure, to demand the reason for such an in-
trusion.

And she froze.

"Hello, Cass," he said quietly. He put out a hand
when she started to rise, casting quick, furious looks
around, searching for someone—one of her watchdogs,
no doubt. "Don't bother to call for help. I came alone.
It's just you and me. I only want to talk."

She sank slowly back into the chair but didn't relax.

"We have nothing to talk about, Corbett Lazlo." Her voice was cold, her eyes hard. "Nothing at all."

"We have a son."

Sparks flared in her eyes, and he saw for a moment the fiery young girl he'd known. "*I* have a son. He is no part of you and you are no part of him. And never will be."

He only shrugged and asked softly, "How is he?"

"He will live—a cripple." Cassandra's voice was a bitter snarl. "*You* did this to him. Are you happy now?"

Corbett shook his head. "You kept his identity from me and from the world. You trained him to be a killer, then turned him loose on his own father. You bear the responsibility for what's happened to him, Cass. You, and no one else."

"You betrayed me!" She surged out of the chair, still gripping its arms as if to stop herself from lunging at his throat. "You made me betray my own father—my brother, my own family."

"Yes, and now I know what it feels like," Corbett said, watching her with narrowed eyes, every nerve in his body on alert. He forced a smile. "You've won, Cass. You've destroyed the agency I built, killed a number of my friends and sent the rest into hiding. And turned someone I trusted against me. So you've done everything you said you'd do, haven't you? You've won. That's what I came to tell you. And to make you a deal."

She straightened to her full height and looked down at him with cold disdain. "What deal could you possibly offer that would interest me? As you say—I have won. You have nothing to deal with. *Nothing.*"

"You're forgetting one thing, aren't you? There's

still the boy. My son." She tensed, and so did he. He saw murder come back into her eyes. "That's right, Cass. He's *my* son, and I want him. I mean to do everything in my power to save him from you. And I'll keep up the fight as long as it takes. Until you, me or both of us are dead. Unless…"

"Unless?" Her voice was as hushed and deadly as a snake's hiss.

Corbett rose to his feet. As tall as she was, he still looked down at her. "I will give up any attempt to win back my son in exchange for two things from you. First, I want your word that you will call off your dogs—leave Lucia Cordez alone."

"Lucia? Oh, yes…" She smiled unpleasantly. "The little computer whiz you are so fond of. The one who shot my son." The smile vanished. "You ask a lot. What is the second thing—perhaps…the moon?"

"No." Now it was he who smiled. He hoped it wasn't a nice smile. "Nothing so romantic. All I want is to know who my betrayer is. Who has been feeding you the inside information that has made it possible for you to destroy the Lazlo Group? I want to hear you say the name."

"You want to know *that?*" Just for a second he saw her gaze flick past him, and her eyes brighten with a terrible gleam of triumph. Then she threw back her head and laughed. His heart hammered in his chest. "You would like to know who betrayed you, Cor-*bey?* That I will tell you—with the greatest pleasure. It was *her,* of course—" She flung out an arm and pointed, with all the dramatic flare of an opera diva. "—the computer genius herself…"

Corbett heard a sharp gasp behind him and spun toward the sound, so that he barely heard the name he'd asked for.

"...*Lucia Cordez.*"

Lucia barely heard the words, either. All she saw was Corbett's face. Corbett's eyes. The fierce blue light of his eyes, and the color draining out of his face.

"Lucia?" It was a question, whispered in disbelief.

She felt frozen, incapable of movement, unable even to shake her head or utter words of reassurance and denial, or even his name. All she could do was lock her eyes with his.

He moved toward her, then, but Cassandra was faster. She sprang, lithe as a panther, and managed to thrust her body between Corbett and Lucia, grab Lucia's arm and turn them both so that she held Lucia in front of her with the arm twisted painfully behind her back.

"Don't struggle," she hissed in Lucia's ear, "or I will kill him where he stands." She reached her free arm around Lucia's side just far enough so that she could see the tiny but lethal gun she held half-concealed in her palm. "And you, Cor-bey," she said, "make one move and I kill her instead. Right in front of your eyes, the way you killed my brother. Of course, I plan to kill her anyway—what did you expect, that I would take your *deal?* Go ahead—try to take your son from me. He hates you now, as much as I do. That is all I care about— that you will never have him. *Never!*"

The guttural shout seemed to hover suspended over the silent trio...until the silence was broken by a word, spoken in a weak voice made harsh by shock and pain.

"*Maman?*" All eyes jerked to the occupant of the

wheelchair rolling soundlessly toward them down the corridor. "Is this true? This man—*est-il mon père?*"

Cassandra gave a gasp that sounded almost like a sob and brought the barrel of the gun up, leveled it, aimed it straight at Corbett. The gunshot that followed blended with a scream of rage and pain, as Lucia stabbed a sewing needle deep into Cassandra's thigh.

Cassandra's wild shot and shouted threats brought the police guard at a dead run with gun drawn. He and Corbett both froze, however, when Cassandra turned the gun and pressed the barrel against Lucia's neck.

Lucia then heard the clatter of running footsteps, but any hopes she might have had of imminent rescue died a moment later when at least half a dozen of Cassandra's armed bodyguards came thundering onto the scene. She could only cling to Corbett's anguished eyes as the uniformed policeman hastily dropped his weapon, and the muscular orderly stepped in front of the wheelchair to shield its vulnerable occupant from flying bullets.

Cassandra's cackle of triumphant laughter had barely faded from Lucia's ears when she heard a loud metallic click very close by. And then a cheerful voice with an unmistakable Australian twang.

"Right-O, Cassandra, m'darlin', that is, indeed, a pistol barrel you feel snuggling up against your pretty head. Now then, I want you to tell all your naughty boys to throw down their toys—there's a good girl."

From what seemed like every corner and nook, every door and corridor in the hospital, came a silent and deadly army, every one of them dressed in black and sporting, on caps, sleeves or jackets, green intertwined pentagrams, the logo of the Lazlo Group.

And then, for the part of the world Lucia occupied, at least, time seemed to stop. All around her was motion, noise, confusion, but where she was…all was silent. Even her heart, her breath was still. She existed in that frozen state like a princess in a fairy tale, cast under a witch's spell, until the voice, the *right* voice…and the touch, the *right* touch, restored her to life again.

"Lucia—my God—"

"Corbett…" Dazed, she put out a hand. Felt stiff fabric, and beneath it the rigid thickness of body armor.

"Lu—are you— God, I thought— I hoped…"

She felt his cheek, bristly with beard, against hers. Heard the tremor in his voice. Her heart began to beat again, hard against the body armor. "Corbett, I'm sorry. I had to come. I found the mole. I'm so sorry. It's—"

"Edward. Yes, I know." His voice was guttural, thick with the grief he couldn't show—not here, not now. Not with his men all around him and an image to uphold.

Lucia, being a woman and therefore not so stupidly constrained, drew a sharp, shuddering breath, buried her face in the warm curve of Corbett's neck and let her tears fall where they pleased.

In the parking lot across the street from the hospital's main entrance, Adam Sinclair leaned against the fender of his BMW and contemplated his future. Time for a change, he thought, watching the couple just now emerging from the revolving doors and making their way down the steps, arms around each other's waists, as if they couldn't bear to be separate from each other even for a moment.

What the hell—he hadn't been home in a while.

Maybe he'd see what sort of excitement Oz had to offer these days.

First, though, there was one last job he had to do—for the Group—and for his oldest and best friend.

He straightened and waved to the couple, who checked then crossed the street to join him, almost running together in perfect step.

"You have him, then?" Corbett asked quietly, not a muscle in his face betraying the emotions Adam knew must be tearing his guts out. Only the diamond hardness of his eyes...

"On ice, back at the shop." Adam tilted his head toward Lucia as he climbed into the driver's seat, but didn't look directly at her. Didn't have to, did he, to know her cheeks were flushed and her eyes gone misty with love. "You want me to get someone to run her home?"

"She comes with me." The simple statement rode over Lucia's sharp intake of breath and told Adam everything he needed to know—if he hadn't already figured it out.

He nodded and turned the ignition key. Corbett and Lucia climbed into the backseat of his car.

At the Lazlo Group's security entrance in the basement parking garage, Corbett took Lucia gently by her arms and looked into her eyes. "Wait for me in the apartment, love. I won't be long. Promise."

"Promise," she whispered.

He kissed her—a much-too-sweet, much-too-brief moment. Then watched her step backward into the elevator. Watched the door whisk silently closed on her somber face and shimmering eyes. Together and in silence, he and Adam waited for the elevator's return. When the door slid open, he placed a hand on Adam's shoulder.

"I think…I have to do this alone," he said in a voice rough with all he couldn't say.

Adam nodded and stepped back. "Gotcha, mate." He held out his hand, grinning crookedly. "I guess it's g'day, then."

Corbett took his hand in a brief, hard grip. Unable to speak, he only nodded, released it and stepped onto the elevator. The door closed, leaving him with a lingering vision of his old friend's face and a sharp sense of loss.

Corbett stepped silently into the steel-walled sound-proof room deep in the bowels of the Lazlo Group's basement keep and closed the door behind him. Hope flashed briefly across the face of the only other person in the room, before a shield of desperate bravado replaced it.

"Corb! What the devil is this all about? I demand—"

"Save it, Edward. I *know*," Corbett replied quietly. He was gratified to discover he felt nothing. Numbness…contempt, perhaps. But that was all. He watched dispassionately as his brother's normally florid face turned pasty, then seemed to collapse in on itself.

"Corb, I swear, I never—"

"I said, save it. I only want to hear enough of your voice to answer me one question. Why'd you do it? Why betray the Group? Why betray *me?*"

"It was that bloody sod, Viktor—he was blackmailing me, Corb. I swear, I had no choice." Edward came toward him, babbling, hands outstretched, entreating. Corbett folded his arms on his chest, barricading himself and his emotions against the onslaught. "I'd got myself in a spot of trouble—my gambling. Look, I'll get help, I swear, I will, if you'll just—"

"People have died, Edward. Good people. People I cared about."

His brother's face spasmed with pain. He drew a shaking hand over his eyes...shook his head. "I never meant to hurt anyone—you must believe that. Least of all you. I thought Viktor only wanted the information to steer clear of our agents...SIS, you know? How was I supposed to know he'd turn around and peddle the stuff to Cassandra DuMont? Viktor promised you'd never be hurt. Devil take him—I *trusted* him, Corb. He was *family.*"

"Family?" It took all the self-control Corbett had to keep his voice quiet. Steady. Rigid as steel. "I'm your family, Eddie. You could have come to me."

"Come to *you?*" Edward halted, his face contorted with anger, eyes filled with tears of resentment, pain. "Mister High-and-Mighty? Mister *Perfect?*" He made a fist and pounded himself in the chest with it. "I'm your big brother! When we were kids, you looked up to *me.* When you were in trouble, you came to *me.* I was the golden boy, not you. And look at you now. You've never set a foot wrong—even that dustup with SIS wasn't your doing. That was the last time I felt like you needed me, wasn't it? You think I don't know you gave me a job out of *pity?* Come to *you* for help? For God's sake, leave me some pride!"

"*Pride*—is that what you call it?" There was no contempt in it, only sadness for all that had been lost. Wasted. Corbett turned, unable to bear looking at his brother's face a moment longer.

"What are you going to do? What's to become of me now?"

Corbett shrugged and said without turning, "As someone once said, frankly, I don't give a damn. You're through with the Lazlo Group, of course. And with me. We'll carry on as usual through Josh and Pru's wedding—I won't spoil that for them, or for Mum and Dad. After that…well, I'll call in a few markers, I suppose, see if I can arrange some kind of deal that might keep you out of jail. If you're willing to tell everything you know about Cass and her operation—and testify against her at trial, of course. After *that,* I don't want to see your face. Ever. Do I make myself clear?"

He waited for the whispered, "Yes," opened the door, then paused. "Oh—and Eddie, you won't make the mistake of trying to run off, will you? Because if you do, I *will* find you. And all bets are off." He went out, leaving his brother standing there. Alone.

Alone.

He stood in the empty corridor…Corbett Lazlo, legendary head of the most respected private-security agency in the world. Powerful…invincible… unknowable. The man in the shadows. Alone.

Except—it came to him then: He didn't have to be alone anymore. And, more important, didn't want to be. He needed…yes, *needed*…warmth, comfort, support. Love. He *needed* with every fiber of his being, every breath in his body. His need overwhelmed him. And his need had a name. *Lucia.*

Lucia. It was true, he didn't just love her, want her. He *needed* her. Needed her with him, supporting him, comforting him, amazing and confounding and exasperating him. Laughing and weeping with him. Making babies with him. Growing old with him.

Halfway down that empty gleaming corridor, Corbett Lazlo began to run.

Epilogue

"*Édesem*... Can you ever forgive me?"

"That depends. Did you really think I could..."

Corbett looked down at the heart-shaped face nestled in the hollow of his shoulder. Luminous eyes gazed back at him, shimmering like quicksilver in the dim light. "Not for even a moment," he said, shaken by the weight and depth of his feelings for her.

"Are you sure?" Her long thick lashes dropped like curtains over her eyes. He felt her deep breath. "Corbett, I saw your face. When she—when Cassandra said that I was—"

"What you saw on my face was sheer horror, no doubt," he said, his voice coming deep and rough from the place inside him that still felt the agony of that moment. "I couldn't believe you were there, after everything I'd done to keep you away."

She sighed again and nestled closer, and he saw a suspicious glimmer under her lashes. "I'm so sorry," she whispered, and the tear quivered free and rolled away down the side of her face and into her hair. Her eyes opened wide again. "*Not* that I came, though—I had to, Corbett. Once I knew. Even though I thought you might never forgive *me*."

"I know," he growled, hugging her close. "I know. I just can't imagine how you managed it. You owe Josef and Kati an enormous apology, you know."

She nodded, sniffed and pulled a hand from under the covers to wipe her eyes. "I'll make it up to them, I swear."

"Kati, especially. You know she thought it was her fault? Evidently, when you went off to the cave to look for your...uh, glasses—supposedly—she thought she had time for a bathroom break. When you didn't show up, she was sure you'd slipped past while she was in the loo. Poor woman was completely distraught."

"Do you think she'll ever forgive me?" Lucia asked in a small voice.

Corbett laughed softly. "Oh, I think she will. Particularly since the subterfuge was done on my behalf."

"It was. Oh, Corbett, I'm so sorry about Edward. When did you know? And how did you figure it out?"

He was silent for a moment, staring up at the stars. Then he drew a breath that pushed against the lingering ache in his ribs and the newer, sharper one in his heart. "Once I forced myself to look at it honestly, it was..." He wouldn't say easy. He wasn't sure he'd ever had anything harder to do in his life. "It was a matter of character—or the lack of it, I suppose. Quite simply, Edward is the only one of you three who's capable of doing such a thing. I think some part of me knew that, just didn't want to believe it. He always was spoiled—had a habit of living beyond his means—and his capabilities. He was the firstborn, the light of our parents' eyes. They'd feared they'd never have kids, you see, and he was their miracle child. Never had to excel, or even try very hard at anything. They treated him like the royal heir no matter what he did. I was rather an afterthought, I think…"

"But…you outdid him in every way. I can't imagine—"

He hugged her closer to silence her, so her next question came muffled and hesitant. "Corbett…what—what will you do about Troy? Now that Cassandra and her thugs have been arrested, what's going to become of him?"

He stirred restlessly, but the knot in his chest stayed where it was. "I called in a few markers. But he's done some terrible things, Lu. How much was his mother's influence and how much his true character—who knows? But once he's out of rehab he's going to prison, there's no way around that, I'm afraid. One good thing—right now he's so angry with Cassandra for lying to him all this time, he may be ready to hear my side of things. Remains to be seen, I guess. He's got a long, hard road to travel."

"He'll make it," Lucia murmured. "He's got you."

"Yes, that he does." He lifted his head to look down at her, and his heart felt as though it had taken up a new position in his throat. "And you? Do we—my son and I—do we have you, as well?" She gazed up at him without speaking. He tried to smile…frowned instead, his breathing, even his heartbeat suspended. "I could use a partner. Particularly now that Adam's decided to go back to Australia."

Smiling to herself in the darkness, Lucia felt overwhelmed with tenderness—not for the powerful, all but invincible leader and teacher she'd always been in awe of, not even for the incredibly skilled and sensitive lover newly met, who turned her bones to warm honey with a touch. But tenderness…for the gentle and vulnerable soul she was only just coming to know. The one who needed her.

She gave a little snort and shifted away from him. "Not interested."

He thought for a moment. "Okay…what about *wife?* As it happens, that position is open, as well."

She turned back to him, eyes narrowed and thoughtful. "Well…that sounds a bit more interesting. Does this…*position* come with benefits?"

"Not very many, I'm afraid," he said somberly. "Just certain…uh, bedroom privileges, and my complete and undying love and utter devotion for the rest of my life.

"That'll do," she said softly.

He leaned down and kissed her a long, lovely time, then leaned back with a sigh. "Plus," he said, nudging her head with his chin, "you get to sleep every night under the stars."

"Yes." Her whispered voice was slurred with tears, but she didn't care if he knew. She had nothing to hide from him, not anymore.

They lay in silence, watching the stars together. Until Lucia tensed suddenly and lifted her head.

"What's that? I swear…I hear…*bells.* Church bells."

After a moment he heard it, too. He lifted his head to look at the clock on the nightstand. "Midnight. Do you suppose…" He lay back, turned to look at her and they said it together.

"It's Christmas!" They touched their smiles together. "Merry Christmas, my—"

"—*édesem,*" she finished for him.

He smiled and kissed her again. "Merry Christmas…*édesem*. My sweet…"

* * * * *

Turn the page for a sneak preview
of the first book in the new miniseries
DIAMONDS DOWN UNDER
from Silhouette Desire®,
VOWS & A VENGEFUL GROOM
by Bronwyn Jameson

Available January 2008
(SD #1843)

Silhouette Desire®
Always Powerful, Passionate and Provocative.

Kimberley Blackstone didn't notice the waiting horde of media until it was too late. Flashbulbs exploded around her like a New Year's light show. She skidded to a halt, so abruptly her trailing suitcase all but overtook her.

This had to be a case of mistaken identity. Surely. Kimberley hadn't been on the paparazzi hit list for close to a decade, not since she'd estranged herself from her billionaire father and his headline-hungry diamond business.

But, no, it was *her* name they called. *Her* face was the focus of a swarm of lenses that circled her like avid hornets. Her heart started to pound with fear-fueled adrenaline.

What did they want?

What was going on?

With a rising sense of bewilderment she scanned the crowd for a clue, and her gaze fastened on a tall, leonine figure forcing his way to the front. A tall, familiar figure. Her head came up in stunned recognition, and their gazes collided across the sea of heads before the cameras erupted with another barrage of flashes, this time right in her exposed face.

Blinded by the flashbulbs—and by the shock of that momentary eye-meet—Kimberley didn't realize his intent until he'd forged his way to her side, possibly by the sheer strength of his personality. She felt his arm wrap around her shoulder, pulling her into the protective shelter of his body, allowing her no time to object. No chance to lift her hands to ward him off.

In the space of a hastily drawn breath, she found herself plastered knee-to-nose against six feet two inches of hard-bodied male.

Ric Perrini.

Her lover for ten torrid weeks, her husband for ten tumultuous days.

Her ex for ten tranquil years.

After all this time, he should not have felt so familiar but, oh dear, he did. She knew the scent of that body and its lean, muscular strength. She knew its heat and its slick power and every response it could draw from hers.

She also recognized the ease with which he'd taken control of the moment and the decisiveness of his deep voice when it rumbled close to her ear. "I have a car waiting outside. Is this your only luggage?"

Kimberley nodded. "I assume you will tell me," she said tightly, "what this welcome party is all about."

"Not while the welcome party is within earshot. No."

Barking a request for the cameramen to stand aside, Perrini took her hand and pulled her into step with his ground-eating stride. Kimberley let him, because he was right, damn his arrogant, Italian-suited hide. Despite the speed with which he whisked her across the airport terminal, she could almost feel the hot breath of the pursuing media on her back.

This was neither the time nor the place for explanations. Inside his car, however, she would get answers.

Now that the initial shock had been blown away—by the haste of their retreat, by the heat of her gathering indignation, by the rush of adrenaline fired by Perrini's presence and the looming verbal battle—her brain was starting to tick over. This had to be her father's doing. And if it was a Howard Blackstone publicity ploy, then it had to be about Blackstone Diamonds, the company that ruled his life.

The knowledge made her chest tighten with a familiar ache of disillusionment.

She'd known her father would be flying in from Sydney for today's opening of the newest in his chain of exclusive, high-end jewelry boutiques. The opulent shopfront sat adjacent to the rival business where Kimberley worked. No coincidence, she thought bitterly, just as it was no coincidence that Ric Perrini was here in Auckland ushering her to his car.

Perrini was Howard Blackstone's right-hand man, second in command at Blackstone Diamonds, a legacy of his short-lived marriage to the boss's daughter. No doubt her father had sent him to fetch her; the question was *why?*

* * * * *

Get swept away down under with the glitz and glamour of the Blackstone empire as Kimberley tries to determine the real reason behind her "reunion" with Ric....

*Look for VOWS & A VENGEFUL GROOM
by Bronwyn Jameson,
in stores January 2008.*

REQUEST YOUR FREE BOOKS!

2 FREE NOVELS PLUS 2 FREE GIFTS!

Silhouette® Romantic

SUSPENSE

Sparked by Danger, Fueled by Passion!

SRS07

Silhouette®

nocturne™

Jachin Black always knew he was an outcast.
Not only was he a vampire, he was a vampire
banished from the Sanguinas society. Jachin, forced
to survive among mortals, is determined to buy
his way back into the clan one day.

Ariel Swanson, debut author of a vampire novel, could
be the ticket he needs to get revenge and take his
rightful place among the Sanguinas again. However,
the unsuspecting mortal woman has no idea of the
dark and sensual path she will be forced to travel.

Look for

RESURRECTION: THE BEGINNING

by

PATRICE MICHELLE

Available January 2008 wherever you buy books.

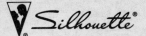

Romantic

SUSPENSE

COMING NEXT MONTH

#1495 FORBIDDEN STRANGER—Marilyn Pappano
When Amanda Nelson sees a Calloway walk into her club, she resists the urge to throw him out. But then she learns Rick isn't really a bartender but an undercover special agent investigating the disappearance of three dancers. Can she trust her greatest enemy… with her life and heart?

#1496 UNDER HIS PROTECTION—Linda Turner
Broken Arrow Ranch
Forced to look after her family's ranch, Elizabeth Wyatt doesn't have time for the arrogant, sexy-as-hell foreman Hunter Sullivan. They both believe they should be in charge. Then strange incidents start to threaten their employees and the land. Now they must join together to save the ranch, while fighting an even deadlier attraction.

#1497 ONE TOUGH AVENGER—Diane Pershing
Lawyer Shannon Coyle is shocked to discover the homeless man she found nearly beaten to death is really CEO Mitch Connor. He has been undercover hoping to find the cult who murdered his wife and child. As Shannon and Mitch work together to unravel a killer's secrets, they also fight a more emotional kind of danger…falling in love.

#1498 COLD CASE COP—Mary Burton
Tara Mackey is a reporter determined to find the missing heiress who vanished on her wedding day. Alex Kirkland is the homicide detective assigned to investigate the disappearance. When Alex learns they must be partners in solving the crime, he doesn't know which is worse— sharing the spotlight...or falling for his new partner.

SRSCNM1207